G000049193

MIDWINTER MYSTERIES
4

MIDWINTER MYSTERIES 4

Edited by
HILARY HALE

LITTLE, BROWN AND COMPANY

A *Little, Brown* Book

First published in Great Britain in 1994
by Little, Brown and Company

A CIP catalogue record for this book
is available from the British Library.

ISBN 0–316–91024–4

Photoset in North Wales by
Derek Doyle & Associates, Mold, Clwyd.
Printed in Great Britain by
Mackays of Chatham PLC, Chatham, Kent

Little, Brown and Company (UK) Limited
Brettenham House
Lancaster Place
London WC2E 7EN

Contents

Contents

Editor's Note

Despite a daily diet of increasing crime statistics, the fictional menu of murder, mayhem and mystery continues to appeal to an ever-widening audience. This is not the place to examine the reasons behind such a phenomenon, indeed the crime fiction addict would probably prefer not to know the result of such a study, but the fact remains that readers thoroughly enjoy the challenge of a genuine puzzle, be it physical or psychological. So it is particularly pleasing to publish an anthology which so perfectly upholds these precepts.

The short story is the most demanding vehicle for a writer to use to satisfy the reader, yet all the contributors to *Midwinter Mysteries 4* have amply displayed their skills in labyrinthine plotting and surprise denouements. Together they have created a volume full of twists and turns and intellectual teases. I would like to thank them all for their individual stories and for collectively giving me so much pleasure in bringing them together.

Hilary Hale

The Gentleman in the Lake

Robert Barnard

The Gentleman in the Lake

There had been violent storms that night, but the body did not come to the surface until they had died down and a watery summer sun sent ripples of lemon and silver across the still-disturbed surface of Derwent Water. It was first seen by a little girl, clutching a plastic beaker of orange juice, who had strayed down from the small car-park, over the pebbles, to the edge of the lake.

'What's that, Mummy?'

'What's what, dear?'

Her mother was wandering round, drinking in the calm, the silence, the magisterial beauty, the more potent for the absence of other tourists. She was a business woman, and holidays by the Lakes made her question uncomfortably what she was doing with her life. She strolled down to where the water lapped on to the stones.

'*There,* Mummy. *That.*'

She looked towards the lake. A sort of bundle bobbed on the surface a hundred yards or so away. She screwed up her eyes. A sort of *tweedy* bundle. Greeny-brown, like an old-fashioned gentleman's suit. As she watched she realised that she could make out, stretching out from the bundle, two lines . . . *legs*. She put her hand firmly on her daughter's shoulder.

'Oh, it's just an old bundle of clothes, darling. Look, there's Patch wanting to play. He has to stretch his legs too, you know.'

Patch barked obligingly, and the little girl trotted off to throw his ball for him. Without hurrying the woman made her way back to the car, picked up the car phone, and dialled 999.

It was late on in the previous summer that Marcia Catchpole had sat beside Sir James Harrington at a dinner party in St John's Wood. 'Something immensely distinguished in law,' her hostess Serena Fisk had told her vaguely. 'Not a Judge, but a rather famous defending counsel, or prosecuting counsel, or something of that sort.'

He had been rather quiet as they all sat down: urbane, courteous in a dated sort of way, but quiet. It was as if he was far away, reviewing the finer points of a case long ago.

'So nice to have *soup,*' said Marcia, famous for 'drawing people out', especially men. 'Soup seems almost to have gone out these days.'

'Really?' said Sir James, as if they were discussing the habits of Eskimos or Trobriand Islanders. 'Yes, I suppose you don't often . . . get it.'

'No, it's all melons and ham, and paté, and seafood cocktails.'

'Is it? *Is* it?'

His concentration wavering he returned to his soup, which he was consuming a good deal more expertly than Marcia, who, truth to tell, was more used to melons and suchlike.

'You don't eat out a great deal?'

'No. Not now. Once, when I was practising . . . But not now. And not since my wife died.'

'Of course you're right: people don't like singles, do they?'

'Singles?'

'People on their own. For dinner parties. They have to find another one – like me tonight.'

'Yes . . . yes,' he said, as if only half-understanding what she said.

'And it's no fun eating in a restaurant on your own, is it?'

'No . . . None at all . . . I have a woman come in,' he added, as if trying to make a contribution of his own.

'To cook and clean for you?'

'Yes . . . Perfectly capable woman . . . It's not the same though.'

'No. Nothing is, is it, when you find yourself on your own?'

'No, it's not . . .' He thought, as if thought was difficult. 'You can't *do* so many things you used to do.'

'Ah, you find that too, do you? What do you miss most?'

There was a moment's silence, as if he had forgotten what they were talking about. Then he said: 'Travel. I'd like to go to the Lakes again.'

'Oh, the Lakes! One of my favourite places. Don't you drive?'

'No. I've never had any need before.'

'Do you have children?'

'Oh yes. Two sons. One in medicine, one in politics. Busy chaps with families of their own. Can't expect them to take me places . . . Don't see much of them . . .' His moment of animation seemed to fade, and he picked away at his entrée. 'What *is* this fish, Molly?'

When the next day she phoned to thank her hostess Marcia commented that Sir James was 'such a sweetie'.

'You and he seemed to get on like a house on fire, anyway.'

'Oh, we did.'

'Other people said he was awfully vague.'

'Oh, it's the legal mind. Wrapped in grand generalities. His wife been dead long?'

'About two years. I believe he misses her frightfully. Molly used to arrange all the practicalities for him.'

'I can believe that. I was supposed to ring him about a book I have that he wanted, but he forgot to give me his number.'

'Oh, it's 271876. A rather grand place in Chelsea.'

But Marcia had already guessed the number after going through the telephone directory. She had also guessed at the name of Sir James's late wife.

'We can't do much till we have the pathologist's report,' said Superintendent Southern, fingering the still-damp material of a tweed suit. 'Except perhaps about *this*.'

Sergeant Potter looked down at it.

'I don't know a lot about such things,' he said, 'but I'd have said that suit was dear.'

'So would I. A gentleman's suit, made to measure and beautifully sewn. I've had one of the secretaries in who knows about these things. A gentleman's suit for country wear. Made for a man who doesn't know the meaning of the word "casual". With a name-tag sewn in by the tailor and crudely removed . . . with a razor-blade probably.'

'You don't *get* razor-blades much these days.'

'Perhaps he's also someone who doesn't know the meaning of the word "throwaway". A picture seems to be emerging.'

'And the removal of the name-tag almost inevitably means—'

'Murder. Yes, I'd say so.'

Marcia decided against ringing Sir James up. She felt sure he would not remember who she was. Instead she would call round with the book, which had indeed come up in conversation – because she had made sure it did. Marcia was very good at fostering acquaintance-ships with men, and had had two moderately lucrative divorces to prove it.

She timed her visit for late afternoon, when she calculated that the lady who cooked and 'did' for him would have gone home. When he opened the door he blinked, and his hand strayed towards his lips.

'I'm afraid I—'

'Marcia Catchpole. We met at Serena Fisk's. I brought the book on Wordsworth we were talking about.'

She proffered Stephen Gill on Wordsworth, in paperback. She had thought as she bought it that Sir James was probably not used to paperbacks, but she decided that, as an investment, Sir James was not yet worth the price of a hardback.

'Oh, I don't . . . er . . . Won't you come in?'

'Lovely!'

She was taken into a rather grim sitting-room, lined with legal books and Victorian first editions. Sir James began to make uncertain remarks about how he thought he could manage tea.

'Why don't you let me make it? You'll not be used to fending for yourself, let alone for visitors. It was different in your generation, wasn't it? Is that the kitchen?'

And she immediately showed an uncanny instinct for finding things and doing the necessary. Sir James watched her, bemused, for a minute or two, then shuffled back to the sitting-room. When she came in with a tray, with tea things on it and a plate of biscuits, he looked as if he had forgotten who she was, and how she came to be there.

'There, that's nice, isn't it? Do you like it strong? Not too strong, right. I think you'll enjoy the Wordsworth book. Wordsworth really *is* the Lakes, don't you agree?'

She had formed the notion, when talking to him at Serena Fisk's dinner party, that his reading was remaining with him longer than his grip on real life. This was confirmed by the conversation on this visit. As long as the talk stayed with Wordsworth and his Lakeland circle it approached a normal chat: he would forget the names of poems, but he would sometimes quote several lines of the better-known ones verbatim. Marcia had been educated at a moderately good state school, and she managed to keep her end up.

Marcia got up to go just at the right time, when Sir James had got used to her being there and before he began wanting her to go. At the door she said: 'I'm expecting to have to go to the Lakes on business in a couple of weeks. I'd be happy if you'd come along.'

'Oh, I couldn't possibly—'

'No obligations either way: we pay for ourselves, separate rooms *of course,* quite independent of each other. I've got business in Cockermouth, and I thought of staying by Buttermere or Crummock Water.'

A glint came into his eyes.

'It would be wonderful to see them again. But I really couldn't—'

'Of course you could. It would be my pleasure. It's always better in congenial company, isn't it? I'll be in touch about the arrangements.'

Marcia was in no doubt she would have to make all the arrangements, down to doing his packing and contacting his cleaning woman. But she was confident she would bring it off.

'Killed by a blow to the head,' said Superintendent Southern, when he had skimmed through the pathologist's report. 'Some kind of accident, for example a boating accident, can't entirely be ruled out, but there was some time between his being killed and his going into the water.'

'In which case, what happened to the boat? And why didn't whoever was with him simply go back to base and report it, rather than heaving him in?'

'Exactly . . . From what remains the pathologist suggests a smooth liver – a townee not a countryman, even of the upper-crust kind.'

'I think you suspected that from the suit, didn't you, sir?'

'I did. Where do you go for a first-rate suit for country

holidays if you're a townee?'

'Same as for business suits? Savile Row, sir?'

'If you're a well-heeled Londoner that's exactly where you go. We'll start there.'

Marcia went round to Sir James's two days before she had decided to set off north. Sir James remembered little or nothing about the proposed trip, still less whether he had agreed to go. Marcia got them a cup of tea, put maps on his lap, then began his packing for him. Before she went she cooked him his light supper (wondering how he had ever managed to cook it for himself) and got out of him the name of his daily. Later on she rang her and told her she was taking Sir James to the Lakes, and he'd be away for at most a week. The woman sounded sceptical but uncertain whether it was her place to say anything. Marcia, in any case, didn't give her the opportunity.

She also rang Serena Fisk to tell her. She had an ulterior motive for doing so. In the course of the conversation she casually asked, 'How did he get to your dinner party?'

'Oh, I drove him. Homecooks were doing the food, so there was no problem. Those sons of his wouldn't lift a finger to help him. Then Bill drove him home later. Said he couldn't get a coherent word out of him.'

'I expect he was tired. If you talk to him about literature you can see there's still a mind there.'

'Literature was never my strong point, Marcia.'

'Anyway, I'm taking him to the Lakes for a week on Friday.'

'*Really*? Well, you are getting on well with him. Rather you than me.'

'Oh, all he needs is a bit of stimulus,' said Marcia. She felt confident now that she had little to fear from old friends or sons.

This first visit to the Lakes went off extremely well from Marcia's point of view. When she collected him the idea that he was going somewhere seemed actually to have got through to him. She finished the packing with last-minute things, got him and his cases into the car, and in no time they were on the M1. During a pub lunch he called her 'Molly' again, and when they at last reached the Lakes she saw that glint in his eye, heard little grunts of pleasure.

She had booked them into Crummock Lodge, an unpretentious but spacious hotel which seemed to her just the sort of place Sir James would have been used to on his holidays in the Lakes. They had separate rooms, as she had promised. 'He's an old friend who's been very ill,' she told the manager. They ate well, went on drives and gentle walks. If anyone stopped and talked Sir James managed a sort of distant benignity which carried them through. As before he was best if he talked about literature. Once, after Marcia had had a conversation with a farmer over a dry stone wall Sir James said, 'Wordsworth always believed in the wisdom of simple country people.'

It sounded like something a school-master had once drummed into him. Marcia would have liked to say, 'But when his brother married a servant he said it was an outrage.' But she herself had risen by marriage, or marriages, and the point seemed to strike too close to home.

On the afternoon when she had her private business in Cockermouth she walked Sir James hard in the morning and left him tucked up in bed after lunch. Then she visited a friend who had retired to a small cottage on the outskirts of the town. He had been a private detective, and had been useful to her in her first divorce. The dicey method he had used to get dirt on her husband had convinced her that in his case private detection was very close to crime itself, and she had maintained the connection. She told him the outline of what she had in mind, and told him she might need him in the future.

When after a week, they returned to London, Marcia was completely satisfied. She now had a secure place in Sir James's life. He no longer looked bewildered when she came round, even looked pleased, and often called her 'Molly'. She went to the Chelsea house often in the evenings, cooked his meal for him, and together they watched television like an old couple.

It would soon be time to make arrangements at a Registry Office.

In the process of walking from establishment to establishment in Savile Row, Southern came to feel he had had as much as he could stand of stiffness, professional discretion and awed hush. They were only high-class tailors, he thought to himself, not the Church of bloody England. Still, when they heard that one of their clients could have ended up as an anonymous corpse in Derwent Water they were willing to co-operate. The three establishments which offered that particular tweed handed him silently a list of those customers who had had suits made from it in the last ten years.

'Would you know if any of these are dead?' he asked

one shop manager.

'Of course, sir. We make a note in our records when their obituary appears in *The Times*.'

The man took the paper back and put a little crucifix sign against two of the four names. The two remaining were a well-known television newsreader and Sir James Harrington.

'Is Sir James still alive?'

'Oh certainly. There's been no obituary for him. But he's very old: we have had no order from him for some time.'

It was Sir James that Southern decided to start with. Scotland Yard knew all about him, and provided a picture, a review of the major trials in which he had featured, and his address. When Southern failed to get an answer from phone calls to the house, he went round to try the personal touch. There was a For Sale notice on it that looked to have been there for some time.

The arrangements for the Registry Office wedding went without a hitch. A month after their trip Marcia went to book it in a suburb where neither Sir James nor she was known. Then she began foreshadowing it to Sir James, to accustom him to the idea.

'Best make it legal,' she said, in her slightly vulgar way.

'Legal?' he enquired, from a great distance.

'You and me. But we'll just go on as we are.'

She thought about witnesses, foresaw various dangers, and decided to pay for her detective friend to come down. He was the one person who knew of her intentions, and he could study Sir James's manner.

'Got a lady friend you could bring with you?' she asked when she rang him.

''Course I have. Though nobody as desirable as you, Marcia love.'

'Keep your desires to yourself, Ben Brackett. This is business.'

Sir James went through the ceremony with that generalised dignity which had characterised him in all his dealings with Marcia. He behaved to Ben Brackett and his lady friend as if they were somewhat dodgy witnesses who happened to be on his side in this particular trial. He spoke his words clearly, and almost seemed to mean them. Marcia told herself that in marrying her he was doing what he actually wanted to do. She didn't risk any celebration after the ceremony. She paid off Ben Brackett, drove Sir James home to change and pack again, then set off for the Lake District.

This time she had rented a cottage, as being more private. It was just outside Grange – a two-bedroomed stone cottage, very comfortable and rather expensive. She had taken it for six weeks in the name of Sir James and Lady Harrington. Once there and settled in Sir James seemed, in his way, vaguely happy: he would potter off on his own down to the lakeside, or up the narrow lanes abutting fields. He would raise his hat to villagers and tourists, and swap remarks about the weather.

He also signed, in a wavering hand, anything put in front of him.

Marcia wrote first to his sons, similar but not identical letters, telling them of his marriage and of his happiness with his dear wife. The letters also touched on business matters: 'I wonder if you would object if I put the house on the market? After living up here I cannot imagine living in London again. Of course the money would come to you after my wife's death.' At the foot of Marcia's typed script Sir James wrote at her direction: 'Your loving Dad.'

The letters brought two furious responses, as Marcia had known they would. Both were addressed to her, and both threatened legal action. Both said they knew their father was mentally incapable of deciding to marry again, and accused her of taking advantage of his senility.

'My dear boys,' typed Marcia gleefully. 'I am surprised that you apparently consider me senile, and wonder how you could have allowed me to live alone without proper care if you believed that to be the case.'

Back and forth the letters flew. Gradually Marcia discerned a subtle difference between the two sets of letters. Those from the MP were slightly less shrill, slightly more accommodating. He fears a scandal, she thought. Nothing worse than a messy court case for an MP's reputation. It was to Sir Evelyn Harrington, MP for Finchingford, that she made her proposal.

Southern found the estate agents quite obliging. Their dealings, they said, had been with Sir James himself. He had signed all the letters from Cumbria. They showed Southern the file, and he noted the shaky signature. They had spoken once to Lady Harrington, they said: a low offer had been received, which demanded a quick decision. They had not recommended acceptance, since, though the property market was more dead than alive, a good house in Chelsea was bound to make a very handsome sum once it picked up. Lady Harrington had said that Sir James had a slight cold, but that he agreed with them that the offer was derisory and should be refused.

Southern's brow creased: wasn't Lady Harrington dead?

There was clearly enough of interest about Sir James Harrington to stay with him for a bit. Southern consulted the file at Scotland Yard and set up a meeting with the man's son at the House of Commons.

Sir Evelyn was a man in his late forties, tall and well-set-up. He had been knighted, Southern had discovered, in the last mass knighting of Tory backbenchers who had always voted at their party's call. The impression Sir Evelyn made was not of a stupid man, but of an unoriginal one.

'My father? Oh yes, he's alive. Living up in the Lake District somewhere.'

'You're sure of this?'

'Sure as one can be when there's no contact.' Southern left a silence, so the man was forced to elaborate. 'Never was much. He's a remote bugger . . . a remote sort of chap, my father. Stiff, always working, never had the sort of common touch you need with children. Too keen on being the world's greatest prosecuting counsel . . . He sent us away to school when we were seven.'

Suddenly there was anger, pain and real humanity in the voice.

'You resented that?'

'*Yes*. My brother had gone the year before, and told me what that prep school was like. I pleaded with him. But he sent me just the same.'

'Did your mother want you to go?'

'My mother did as she was told. Or else.'

'That's not the present Lady Harrington?'

'Oh no. The present Lady Harrington is, I like to think, what my father deserves . . . We'd been warned he was failing by his daily. Dinner burnt in the oven, forgetting to change his clothes, that kind of thing. We didn't take too much notice. The difficulties of getting a stiff-necked old . . . man into residential care seemed insuperable. Then the next we heard he's married again and gone to live in the Lake District.'

'Didn't you protest?'

'Of course we did. It was obvious she was after his money. And the letters he wrote, or she wrote for him, were all wrong. He would *never* have signed himself Dad, let alone 'Your loving Dad'. But the kind of action that would have been necessary to annul the marriage can look ugly – for *both* sides of the case. So when she proposed an independent examination by a local doctor and psychiatrist I persuaded my brother to agree.'

'And what did they say?'

'Said he was vague, a little forgetful, but perfectly capable of understanding what he'd done when he married her, and apparently very happy. That was the end of the matter for us. The end of *him*.'

Marcia had decided from the beginning that in the early months of her life as Lady Harrington she and Sir James would have to move around a lot. As long as he was merely an elderly gentleman pottering around the Lakes and exchanging meteorological banalities with the locals there was little to fear. But as they became used to him there was a danger that they would try to engage him in conversation of more substance. If that happened his mental state might very quickly become apparent.

As negotiations with the two sons developed Marcia began to see her way clear. Their six weeks at Grange were nearing an end, so she arranged to rent a cottage between Crummock Water and Cockermouth. When the sons agreed to an independent assessment of their father's mental condition and nominated a doctor and a psychiatrist from Keswick to undertake it, Marcia phoned them and arranged their visit for one of their first days in the new cottage. Then she booked Sir James and herself into Crummock Lodge for the relevant days. 'I'll be busy getting the cottage ready,' she told the manager. She felt distinctly pleased with herself. No danger of the independent team talking to locals.

'I don't see why we have to move,' complained Sir James when she told him. 'I like it here.'

'Oh, we need to see a few places before we decide where we really want to settle,' said Marcia soothingly. 'I've booked us into Crummock Lodge, so I'll be able to get the new cottage looking nice before we move in.'

'This is nice. I want to stay here.'

There was no problem with money. On a drive to Cockermouth Marcia had arranged to have Sir James's bank account transferred there. He had signed the form without a qualm, together with one making the account a joint one. Everything in the London house was put into store, and the estate agents forwarded Sir James's mail, including his dividend cheques and his pension, regularly. There was no hurry about selling the house, but when it did finally go Marcia foresaw herself in clover. With Sir James, of course, and he was a bit of a bore. But very much worth putting up with.

As Marcia began discreetly packing for the move Sir James's agitation grew, his complaints became more insistent.

'I don't want to move. Why should we move, Molly? We're happy here. If we can't have this cottage we can buy a place. There are houses for sale.'

To take his mind off it Marcia borrowed their neighbour's rowing boat and gave him a little trip on the lake. It didn't take his mind off it. 'This is lovely,' he kept saying. 'Derwent Water has always been my favourite. Why should we move on? I'm not moving, Molly.'

He was beginning to get on her nerves. She had to tell herself that a few frazzled nerves were a small price to pay.

The night before they were due to move the packing had to be done openly. Marcia brought all the suitcases into the living-room and began methodically distributing to each one the belongings they had brought with them. Sir James had been dozing when she began, as he often did in the evening. She was half-way through her task when she realised he was awake and struggling to his feet.

'You haven't been listening to what I've been saying, have you, Molly? Well, have you, woman? I'm not moving!'

Marcia got to her feet.

'I know it's upsetting, dear—'

'It's not upsetting because we're staying here.'

'Perhaps it will only be for a time. I've got it all organised, and you'll be quite comfy—'

'Don't treat me like a child, Molly!' Suddenly she

realised with a shock that he had raised his arm. 'Don't treat me like a child!' His hand came down with a feeble slap across her cheek. 'Listen to what I say, woman!' Slap again. 'I am not moving!' This time he punched her, and it hurt. 'You'll do what I say, or it'll be the worse for you!' And he punched her again.

Marcia exploded with rage.

'You *bloody* old bully!' she screamed. 'You brute! That's how you treated your wife, is it? Well, it's not how you're treating me!'

She brought up her stronger hands and gave him an almighty shove away from her even as he raised his fist for another punch. He lurched back, tried to regain his balance, then fell against the fireplace, hitting his head hard against the corner of the mantelpiece. Then he crumpled to the floor and lay still.

For a moment Marcia did nothing. Then she sat down and sobbed. She wasn't a sobbing woman, but she felt she had had a sudden revelation of what this man's – this old monster's – relations had been with his dead wife. She had never for a moment suspected it. She no longer felt pity for him, if she ever had. She felt contempt.

She dragged herself wearily to her feet. She'd put him to bed, and by morning he'd have forgotten. She bent down over him. Then, panic-stricken, she put her hand to his mouth, felt his chest, felt for his heart. It didn't take long to tell that he was dead. She sat down on the sofa and contemplated the wreck of her plans.

Southern and Potter found the woman in the general-store-cum-newsagent's at Grange chatty and informative.

'Oh, Sir James. Yes, they were here for several weeks. Nice enough couple, though I think he'd married beneath him.'

'Was he in full possession of his faculties, do you think?'

The woman hesitated.

'Well, you'd have thought so. Always said "Nice day" or "Hope the rain keeps off" if he came in for a tin of tobacco or a bottle of wine. But no more than that. Then one day I said "Shame about the Waleses, isn't it?" – you know, at the time of the split-up. He seemed bewildered, and I thought he imagined I was talking about whaling or something, so I said "The Prince and Princess of Wales separating." Even then it was obvious he didn't understand. It was embarrassing. I turned away and served somebody else. But there's others had the same experience.'

After some minutes Marcia found it intolerable to be in the same room as the body. Trying to look the other way she dragged it through to the dining-room. Even as she did so she realised that she had made a decision: she was not going to the police, and her plans were not at an end.

Because after all she had her 'Sir James' all lined up. In the operation planned for the next few days the existence of the real one was anyway something of an embarrassment. Now that stumbling-block had been removed. She rang Ben Brackett and told him there had been a slight change of plan, but it needn't affect his part in it. She rang Crummock Lodge and told them that Sir James had changed his mind and wanted to settle straight into the new cottage. While there was still some dim light she went into the garden and out into the lonely land behind, collecting as many large stones as she could find. Then she slipped down and put them into the rowing-boat she had borrowed from her neighbour the day before.

She had no illusions about the size – or more specifically the weight – of the problem she had in disposing of the body. She gave herself a stiff brandy, but no more than one. She found a razor-blade and, shaking, removed the name from Sir James's suit. Then she finished her packing, so that everything was ready for departure. The farming people of the area were early to bed as a rule, but there were too many tourists staying there, she calculated, for it to be really safe before the early hours. At precisely one o'clock she began the long haul down to the shore. Sir James had been nearly six foot, so though his form was wasted he was both heavy and difficult to lift. Marcia found, though, that carrying was easier than dragging, and quieter too. In three arduous stages she got him to the boat, then into it. The worst was over. She rowed out to the dark centre of the lake – the crescent moon was blessedly obscured by clouds – filled his pockets with stones, then carefully, gradually, eased the body out of the boat and into the water. She watched it sink, then made for the shore. Two large brandies later she piled the cases into the car, locked up the cottage, and drove off in the Cockermouth direction.

After the horror and difficulty of the night before everything went beautifully. Marcia had barely settled into the new cottage when Ben Brackett arrived. He already had some of Sir James's characteristics off pat: his distant, condescending affability, for example. Marcia coached him in others, and they tried to marry them to qualities the real Sir James had no longer had: lucidity and purpose.

When the team of two arrived the fake Sir James was working in the garden. 'Got to get it in some sort of order,' he explained, in his upper-class voice. 'Haven't the strength I once had, though.' When they were all inside, and over a splendid afternoon tea, he paid eloquent tribute to his new wife.

'She's made a new man of me,' he explained. 'I was letting myself go after Molly died. Marcia pulled me up in my tracks and brought me round. Oh, I know the boys are angry. I don't blame them. In fact, I blame myself. I was never a good father to them – too busy to be one. Got my priorities wrong. But it won't hurt them to wait a few more years for the money.'

The team was clearly impressed. They steered the talk round to politics, the international situation, changes in the law. 'Sir James' kept his end up, all in that rather grand voice and distant manner. When the two men left, Marcia knew that her problems were over. She and Ben Brackett waited for the sound of the car leaving to go back to Keswick, then she poured very large whiskies for them. Over their third she told him what had happened to the real Sir James.

'You did superbly,' said Ben Brackett when she had finished.

'It was bloody difficult.'

'I bet it was. But it was worth it. Look how it went today. A piece of cake. We had them in the palms of our hands. We won, Marcia! Let's have another drink on that. We won!'

Even as she poured Marcia registered disquiet at that 'we'.

*

Sitting in his poky office in Kendal, Southern and Potter surveyed the reports and other pieces of evidence they had set out on the desk.

'It's becoming quite clear,' said Southern thoughtfully. 'In Grange we have an old man who hardly seems to know who the Prince and Princess of Wales are. In the cottage near Cockermouth we have an old man who can talk confidently about politics and the law. In Grange we have a feeble man, and a corpse which is that of a soft liver. In the other cottage we have a man who gardens – perhaps to justify the fact that his hands are *not* those of a soft-living lawyer. At some time between taking her husband on the Lake – was that a rehearsal, I wonder? – and the departure in the night, she killed him. She must already have had someone lined up to take his place for the visit of the medical team.'

'And they're there still,' said Potter, pointing to the letter from the estate agents in London. 'That's where all communications still go.'

'And that's where we're going to go,' said Southern, getting up.

They had got good information on the cottage from the Cockermouth police. They left their car in the car-park of a roadside pub, and took the lane through fields and down towards the northern shore of Crummock Water. They soon saw the cottage, overlooking the Lake, lonely . . .

But the cottage was not as quiet as its surroundings. As they walked towards the place they heard shouting. A minute or two later they heard two thick voices, arguing. When they could distinguish words it was in a voice far from upper-crust:

'Will you get that drink, you cow? . . . How can I when I can hardly stand? . . . Get me that drink or it'll be the worse for you tomorrow . . . You'd better remember who stands between you and a long jail sentence, Marcia. You'd do well to think about that *all the time* . . . Now get me that Scotch or you'll feel my fist!'

When Southern banged on the door there was silence. The woman who opened the door was haggard-looking, with bleary eyes and a bruise on the side of her face. In the room behind her, slumped back in a chair, they saw a man whose expensive clothes were in disarray, whose face was red and puffy, and who most resembled a music hall comic's version of a gentleman.

'Lady Harrington? I'm Superintendent Southern and this is Sergeant Potter. I wonder if we could come in? We have to talk to you.'

He raised his ID towards her clouded eyes. She looked down at it slowly. When she looked up again Southern could have sworn that the expression on her face was one of relief.

The Perfect Way to Murder Your Spouse

Brian Battison

The Perfect Way to Murder Your Spouse

Barry Edmond knew the precise moment when he had decided to kill his wife; that beautiful split-second when fantasy and reality had merged.

The fantasies had begun two years after his marriage. Often, when he appeared for all the world to be absorbed in the television screen, he would in fact be visualising some horrible form of death for his wife.

For a long time his favourite had been a variation on an American Indian method he had once read about. He couldn't for the life of him remember which tribe instilled this particular form of torture but he did know that they must have hated their enemies just as much as he hated Susan.

As a prelude to his own delightful form of torment, he would imagine the braves, clad only in dirty loin-cloths, pulling an unfortunate settler from his home; the muscles of their magnificent torsos rippling as they staked the man of Polish descent (he was always Polish because Susan was of Polish descent) to the ground.

The man, writhing and screaming in anticipation of the pain that was to come, would watch as rawhide ropes, soaked in water, were secured to his wrists and ankles, then attached to posts driven into the ground. In the powerful sunlight the ropes would eventually dry and contract, pulling his limbs from their sockets in the process.

Now your ordinary hater would probably be content to leave it there, but not Barry's red devils; with their victim nicely suffering, they would gleefully build a fire on his chest, chat away in an extremely friendly fashion, and make wagers as to whether the fire would reach his heart before his legs and arms were pulled off.

Not that Barry seriously considered this to be a suitable death for Susan, but for a while it had to suffice because, try as he might, he could think of nothing more horrific.

Those imagined sun-baked plains with the long grasses dancing to the wind were now replaced by the oil-stained floor of Barry's garage . . . with Susan staked out on it. Barry could see himself systematically driving their Ford Escort over her arms and legs, then straight up the centre of her body until one of the wheels rested directly below her chin.

He never questioned how he would manoeuvre the car within the confines of the garage, or indeed why his wife did not die in the process, for she was always alive when he crawled under the car and lit a cigarette by her side.

Susan, her lips almost unable to form the words because of her severe pain, would croak, 'Don't smoke, Barry, it makes the house smell.'

But he would smoke, and he would flick the ash into her pale cracked face until the stub was so short it burnt his fingers. Only then would he climb back into the car and very slowly and very deliberately drive over Susan's face.

For five years, this fantasy and others like it had provided Barry with a useful avenue along which to channel his hatred.

Not that he had always been unhappy; it just seemed that way.

Barry wasn't the material from which Hollywood legends were made but – as his mother always said – in his younger days he had been quite presentable and had possessed enough sense to only target girls with whom no other men would have bothered. This willingness not to be over fussy had led to many a happy dalliance (in dimly lit venues) along life's path during his adolescence and early manhood.

It was at the age of twenty-five, as he was trundling along that well-worn route, that he encountered Susan.

For Barry it was lust at first sight. And as Susan was two years older she had the added attraction of being the Older Woman. Susan was definitely a digression from Barry's norm.

For some reason his six-foot frame had always attracted – well, there's no point in trying to be kind about this – rather short, dumpy girls.

One of his more painful memories of B.S. (Before Susan) involved his father and a girl called Carol.

Barry had at last reached the landmark age of

eighteen and Carol was his first real girlfriend. She stood four foot eleven in her tights, but her lack of stature was more than compensated for in other directions.

Barry's belief that his father was a rather uncouth individual proved to be well-founded when – even though he had reached manhood and felt he could demand a little respect from those around him, and even though he had started to use Old Spice aftershave – his dear old dad took to seeing them off whenever they left the family home.

He would stand there on the doorstep, watching Barry gallantly opening the passenger door for Carol, and call out wickedly, 'Have you got your steps with you, love . . . to stand on when you kiss him goodnight?'

Barry could never understand why his father had laughed so loudly at his so-called joke; Barry hadn't found it in the least funny. But that episode had stayed with him; even now he walked with a slight stoop which had begun as an unconscious effort to appear shorter.

However, Susan was a vision: five foot ten of willowy blonde. Her facial bone-structure was so fine that she could not help but look enigmatic.

In the normal run of things Barry would have considered her to be out of his league, and rather than face a humiliating rejection, would have left her alone.

Susan's approach to selecting a partner was not dissimilar to his own, however, and she considered Barry to be suitable husband fodder: not good-looking; neither intelligent nor good company – perfect material from which to shape a husband and provider.

Susan knew that her looks and sexual skills would not bewitch him forever, but even when familiarity bred discontent, he would be unlikely to stray into exciting adventures because no other woman would look at him.

By modern day standards she had made Barry wait to sample her body; despite his most persistent efforts she had not succumbed until the fifth date.

The back seat of a battered Cortina on a freezing cold November night does not create conditions conducive to the earth moving, but after a great deal of violent and fervent effort on both their parts, it managed to give a sensuous shudder.

Barry misinterpreted this as love.

Now any rational, clear-thinking male would have accepted Susan's explanation that her wide knowledge of sexual practices and her ever-willingness to take the lead was due entirely to the fact that she was a natural lover, put on this earth to please just one man – Barry.

Unfortunately, however many times Susan explained this to Barry, she could not shake his conviction that she'd had a wide and varied string of lovers before they had met. This in turn led to a great deal of insecurity within him which manifested itself in jealous rages every time another man so much as looked at her.

The incident with the traffic warden finally brought home to Barry the need to control this impetuous nature.

The warden in question was handing Susan a ticket for parking on double yellow lines when an enraged Barry pushed between them, demanding to be told how long they had been seeing each other.

With polite firmness the warden tried to intervene in

the ensuing argument, only to be punched in the eye by Barry and sustaining a wound which needed six stitches to stem the flow of blood.

However much Susan and Susan's parents and Barry's parents reasoned with him, they could not shake his belief that the parking ticket had been a form of coded message, informing Susan of the place at which to meet the man for a bout of illicit lovemaking.

Barry did, however, take his solicitor's advice. A kindly man, the solicitor said that, although he agreed that this was a plausible explanation, he did not feel totally happy about putting it before a court of law as a mitigating circumstance – especially as the prosecution were claiming that the warden had been impotent for the last ten years.

Barry pleaded guilty, was called a silly young man by the magistrate, and was fined five hundred pounds plus costs.

In retrospect, Barry could see that even then Susan had begun to take charge of his life. He needed to smarten himself up, she said; needed to change his hairstyle, get himself noticed in life. The promotion ladder, she explained, was difficult to get on to but once a foothold had been gained, the only way was up.

Barry's job was to put packets of washing powder into new washing machines before they left the factory. Hardly an exacting exercise, but one in which he was quite happy.

Yet within six months of Susan taking over his push to the top, he had risen to the post of supervisor – now his main responsibility was to ensure that other workers put the packets of washing powder into the machines correctly.

To celebrate his promotion, Barry and Susan were married. They settled down in a small three-bedroomed semi-detached on Denmark Hill (re-named Crash Hill by the locals, due to the fact that it was situated at the top of a steep incline which led down to a motorway junction, and was notorious for the amount of crashes that occurred there in bad weather).

It soon became clear that the changes in Barry's appearance were only the start; Susan no longer liked him to smoke – although she had never objected before the wedding – because it was distasteful and vulgar.

Barry stood his ground there (well, almost); he did cut down the number of cigarettes he smoked, especially in the house, but he still had one with his morning coffee before work, and when he came home in the evening he would place his Tupperware sandwich container on the hall table and light one up then.

During those first two years of married life it became apparent to Barry that his wife was one of those people who skips from subject to subject, fad to fad. Wholemeal bread; lettuce with every meal; fat-free this; fat-free that; sweeteners instead of sugar.

Eggs, bacon, black pudding and fried bread vanished from Barry's world. He complained bitterly but Susan remained adamant. Those things were bad for him, she said; so was the vast amount of lager he was in the habit of consuming; far better to cut that out too, and with the money saved they could buy bottled mineral water.

Barry couldn't see the sense in giving up the lager he enjoyed so much to buy bottled water which seemed exactly the same as the stuff from the tap.

His trips to the pub became less frequent.

It was about this time that he began to fantasise – not about actually murdering Susan, but about re-establishing his male dominance.

Harmless little flights of fancy really, like leaving her chained up when he left for work, then coming home at night to smoke five cigarettes, consume an enormous fry-up washed down with six pints of lager, before beating her repeatedly with a cane and then venting his lust on her.

Afterwards she would feed him grapes, lovingly kissing each one before placing it to his lips, and making sure that his pint glass was never more than half empty. It was a little trick that added a bit of sparkle to a flagging sex life.

Then Susan became a feminist.

At first Barry did not realise the implications, but they were brought home to him with amazing speed.

'New woman', it seemed, was far more butch than 'down-trodden woman'. Susan took to wearing a baseball cap and jeans and referred to her group of seven like-minded females as 'the guys'.

They met at each other's houses on a rota basis. It took only two such meetings, held at his house over a space of fourteen weeks, for Barry to realise that his marriage was in real trouble.

He arrived home one evening, put his Tupperware sandwich container on the hall table and was lighting a cigarette when he heard female voices coming from the lounge.

A flustered Susan emerged. 'Put that bloody thing out,' she hissed. 'You show me up. That's all you do – you show me up!'

Barry simply stood there, open-mouthed, obediently stubbing out his cigarette while Susan continued with her whispered onslaught.

'I've done a buffet for the guys. Get in there and circulate, for God's sake, they'll think you're anti-social.'

Barry, although he did his best, could not carry it off with his usual aplomb. Of the seven women standing about, eating sausages on sticks, he chose the one who, apart from her white skin, was a dead ringer for Mike Tyson and attempted to strike up a conversation.

'Hi,' he said, thinking how trendy he sounded. 'I'm Barry – Susan's husband.'

'I'm Sharon,' the woman answered in a gravel voice, 'and I think I should make it plain from the start that I think all men are pigs.'

After that Barry tried to steer the conversation on to a neutral subject – England's dismal showing in the World Cup. He was glad when the buffet tea was over.

The next time the meeting was held at his home he was determined to miss it. He smoked his cigarette in the garage before letting himself quietly into the house, intending to creep upstairs and remain in the bedroom until the meeting was over.

So intent was he on not being noticed that it took a couple of seconds for the words to sink in. As they did he stopped and crouched on the stairs, listening to the sounds coming through the lounge door which was slightly ajar.

'For fifteen years I've had to put up with it. Marriage isn't the right term for it – a sentence, more like.'

The murmurs of approval greeting this remark seemed to spur the speaker on.

'The washing, cooking, keeping the house clean, I can cope with. But what I can't – and pray God and you guys can give me the strength not to tolerate it much longer – is that filthy pig degrading and defiling me three times a week.'

Above sympathetic noises, the voice of Mike Tyson's look-alike rose. 'Thank you, Janine. We feel deeply for you. Susan, do you want to speak?'

Susan did. She began, 'One of our aims is to support each other – right?'.

Barry had noticed of late that many of Susan's statements were ending in 'right?'

'Well, you guys have supported me without knowing it. Before this meeting I thought I was the only woman who felt that way – right? I thought women were supposed to enjoy sex and that I'd just been unfortunate in my choice of pig. Often, after the so-called pleasurable event I've lain there thinking: Barry, you're about as much use as a cheese sandwich in a wet dream.'

This brought the house down. And most of it seemed to be crashing around Barry's ears; so much so that he missed Susan's closing remark.

Then somebody said, 'That's good, guys. However oppressed we are, we mustn't lose our sense of humour – right?'

Quite understandably, after that assessment of his performance, Barry found the act of sexual intercourse somewhat hard to sustain, which did nothing to improve his temper. During the next few weeks there were many at the washing machine factory going home at night wondering why, after years of putting washing powder in the machines, they had suddenly started to do it wrong.

*

Three weeks later, after another meeting with the guys, Susan strode into the lounge and stood defiantly in front of the fireplace.

Barry watched as she pushed the baseball cap to the back of her head and hooked her thumbs into the tops of her jeans – at any moment he expected her to spit in the grate.

She didn't. Instead, she said, 'Diana says that any woman who's asked to have sexual intercourse is technically being raped. I agree. I am now giving you warning that you will never rape me again. Not while I'm alive – you'll have to kill me first.'

Then she turned and fled from the room, obviously in an emotional state.

Barry stayed in the chair for some time. Upstairs he could hear Susan sobbing her heart out.

Try as he might he could not help feeling that he was being wrongly accused. What about all the times he had felt Susan's leg creeping across him as she pulled herself on top? The times she had whispered tauntingly, 'I bet you can't do it a third time . . . I just bet you can't.'

In a way, though, the cessation of their sexual activities was a relief.

Over the next six months they spent a lot of time under the same roof without actually living together.

Barry hardly noticed that the baseball cap and jeans had given way to quite short dresses and a feature-softening hairstyle.

'I've joined an amateur dramatic group,' Susan announced one evening.

As the rest of the television-viewing population was enthralled by events taking place in *Coronation Street*, Barry was watching himself on the screen, attempting to drive a sharpened stake through Susan's heart; he aborted the exercise, however, on the grounds that it was a far too humane form of execution.

He was examining the possibilities of a chain-saw when Susan repeated, 'I've joined an amateur dramatic group,' in her you're-not-listening-and-I'm-getting-annoyed voice.

'Good,' Barry mumbled.

'I had an audition and the director said I was very talented,' she told him proudly.

'Good.'

'And then he gave me the lead in *Romeo and Juliet*.'

Susan studied him for some reaction to the news that he was married to an aspiring actress.

Barry realised only too well that his conversational powers were becoming stilted but, again, all he could say was, 'Good.'

So the play became the thing.

At first Susan's absences three times a week for rehearsals were like a warm wind of happiness blowing through the house. But then Barry realised that for the fantasies to work her presence was required, because even after he had murdered her twice in quick succession, the slightest glance at her could help rekindle the hatred inside and inspire him to more horrific deeds.

Barry became bored.

Out of that boredom sprang an idea that divorce might be his salvation. He studied books on the subject from the library but found only disillusionment: from what he could glean, if they were to divorce, Susan would walk away with half the house, half the furniture, half the car, and also half the money *they* had saved by Barry's drastic cut-backs in lager swilling and tobacco consumption.

Still, he flirted with the idea; it seemed reasonable and acceptably cost effective. After all, they still owed a lot on the mortgage, so Susan would get half of what?

The more he considered it, the more of a possibility it became. He would quickly recover, he thought reassuringly, set himself up in a nice little smokers' zone, and enjoy his freedom.

But then this lifeline was cut by further study. It seemed that Susan would be able to claim a third of Barry's income for the rest of his working life. So that would mean living in a crummy bed-sit, working all hours God sent, and supporting her for years to come.

The door shut firmly on divorce . . . only to re-open again.

Susan began to arrive home later and later from rehearsals. During the first week she was back by 10:15; by the third week it was nearer 12:25. Always she had lifts home in a red Metro.

An affair. Barry grasped at the idea as a drowning man does at a straw.

If the Metro man was so infatuated with Susan he might be willing to take her off Barry's hands, in return for half the furniture etcetera, and forgo the third of his so far unearned income.

When Susan came in on Thursday night – or to be more precise, Friday morning – Barry was waiting up for her. 'Who was that in the Metro?' he asked casually.

'Simon Shafton.' She sounded shifty.

'Not having an affair with him, are you?'

'Don't start that, Barry,' she flared; her new-found artistic temperament spilling over. 'I still haven't forgotten the traffic warden. The look on that poor man's face when you hit him . . . it was so embarrassing.'

'Only joking,' Barry laughed.

Not wishing to overplay his hand, he began to make her a cup of tea.

'Si's sweet,' Susan enthused. 'He's Romeo, by the way. God, he brings depth and feeling to the part. Sometimes, when I'm on stage with him I can feel his talent consuming me . . .' For some reason, with arms hugging her chest, she did a dramatic tour of the kitchen. ' . . . but like all stars, he's difficult. Sent the director mad at the blocking rehearsal.'

Blocking, Barry discovered – between stifling yawns – was when the director tells his cast where to stand and when to move.

Romeo Shafton, it seemed, had two moles on his left cheek, and although these were hardly visible, Si – poor love – had developed such a thing about them that he would only show his right profile to the adoring fans. Barry had little knowledge of things theatrical, but even he could see the problems this could cause even the most patient of directors.

Listening to Susan now, Barry knew that the possibility of her having an affair was good. If this doesn't work, he thought (only half-jokingly), I shall *have* to murder her.

As opening nights go, it was a disaster.

Barry, together with forty others – all relatives of the cast – was jammed into a small hall at the Co-Op.

From her very first line, it was obvious that Susan did not possess even a modicum of acting talent. And at thirty-five years of age she brought an almost geriatric touch to the role of Juliet, for the harsh stage lights seemed to highlight every tiny wrinkle and flaw on her face.

Wooden she was not; she delivered every line with a force which suggested that the very future of the world depended on it, and gesticulated wildly at every opportunity.

Simon Shafton, who appeared to be grossly short-sighted, turned in a moderately good – if one-sided – performance.

Then, thankfully, after the company had taken countless curtain calls to a smattering of applause, it was all over.

Barry sat waiting in the draughty room.

Susan burst in, still playing to the departing audience. 'Darling,' she said, 'we're having champagne and a first night bash backstage, so you can go home. Si will give me a lift back.'

As he drove up Crash Hill, a plan was formulating in Barry's mind, but first he would need proof that Susan was involved in an affair. Once he had that he would be perfectly reasonable about it all.

But he knew that time was of the essence; he must strike while the passion was hot. So many things could go wrong: Susan could tire of Simon; he could tire of her; the man could get his eyes tested – any one of a number of things could happen.

His chance came the following week.

It was Tuesday evening. As he put his Tupperware sandwich container on the hall table and lit a cigarette, Susan appeared in the kitchen doorway and announced that the group had decided to hold four post-play meetings, to discuss individual performances: two this week; two, next.

Barry knew it was a lie. It just wasn't humanly possible to discuss all that went wrong with *Susan's* performance in four evenings, let alone those of the whole cast.

Barry decided to follow her.

By the time he had the Escort out of the garage, Shafton's Metro was almost out of sight, and Barry really had to put his foot down – a dangerous thing to do on Crash Hill. But he caught up and tucked himself in some thirty yards behind.

Disappointment washed over him on realising that they were, after all, heading for the Co-Op Hall. There really was a meeting. Despondently he watched them drive into the car-park.

Barry had stopped the car, was about to reverse and go home, when he noticed there were no lights on in the hall, and his heartbeat quickened considerably when he realised that the Metro had gone into a car-park beyond the car-park; a secluded area large enough for twenty cars, surrounded by trees and bushes.

After parking the Escort he ran the thirty yards to the hall, arriving breathlessly. With chest heaving, he stealthily crossed the main car-park and peered through the bushes.

Susan and Simon were locked in what a divorce

lawyer would describe as 'a fiery embrace' in the back of the Metro.

Fascinated, Barry watched as Susan tore at Simon's lap and pulled down his trousers. Then Simon, turning to his left and favouring Susan with his best side, settled back in the seat as she clambered on top.

'The swine's raping her,' Barry thought with just a trace of irony.

Gradually the sight of his wife gyrating up and down on Shafton's prostrate form began to fade as the car windows steamed up, but not before a feeling had begun to grow inside him; it was so violent, so unexpected, that he had to turn away, unable to watch any longer.

Barry ran back to his car and by the time he had unlocked the door, his emotions were once again in check.

He would refuse to let sympathy for Simon Shafton stand in his way. The man was old enough to know what he was letting himself in for . . . and, after all, he'd be getting half the furniture etcetera.

Watching Susan fulfilling her most basic urge had had a strange effect on Barry; it had awakened his own latent sex drive, which had been put on ice because he had felt it was the primary cause of his downfall; but now, reactivated, it needed to be satisfied.

And would not a sexual conquest make him feel like a man again; fortified for the task ahead?

Carrie was a nice girl; all the men said so.

Her job was to ascertain that there was enough washing powder in each box before they were passed on to the operatives who placed them in the machines. She carried out the job with great diligence.

Carrie was the sort of girl a man would not be ashamed to be seen out with – all the men said so. And she was not averse to removing her undergarments once primed with sufficient rum and peppermint. Indeed, by the time Carrie had consumed enough to carry out the happy task she was probably unaware that she was doing it.

Barry took her to the Dog & Duck public house and plied her with the necessary amount of alcoholic beverage.

He sneered slightly at Simon Shafton's lack of taste – the car-park at the Co-Op indeed!

Barry had far more style. He took Carrie back to the factory and warmed sacks on the radiators before spreading them on the concrete floor.

Carrie's reactions to his lovemaking told him he had lost none of his old skills. She was limp, pacific, but the rapidity with which she breathed caused a sensuous snorting sound in her throat . . . similar to a snore.

When he felt the moment of climax approaching Barry had the manners to whisper, 'Thank you, Carrie, thank you,' to heighten her pleasure.

This brought forth much snorting and when it was over Barry was filled with a tenderness he had never before felt for a woman.

In repose Carrie's fulfilment was evident; her nostrils flared, her lips trembled – she looked so happy, so peaceful, she could almost have been asleep.

It took her some time to emerge from this trance-like state which Barry's expert lovemaking had induced. And when she finally did, it was with a start; almost as if she had no idea where she was.

Three repeats, performed on consecutive evenings

were enough to restore Barry's masculinity to the point where he felt able to confront Susan with his proposal.

His timing, he reasoned, could not have been better. Shafton had been away for a week, guesting for another drama group, so Susan hadn't seen him for seven whole days. He was due back today, and the care with which she showered and dressed indicated that a steamy reunion was very much on the cards.

While Susan was out, Barry sampled the Scotch he had bought from an off-licence on the way home, and by the time Susan's key turned in the lock, he had consumed far more than had been intended. Still, he knew that the light-headed, dizzy feeling he was experiencing would not affect his performance – unless, of course, he tried to stand up and move about.

Susan swept into the room. 'Hello, darling,' she said happily. The 'darling' was not a term of endearment; of late she addressed everyone in that way.

'Susan,' Barry said, keeping his voice steady, 'sit down. I want to talk to you.'

'You've been drinking,' she said, facing him across the kitchen table.

He looked at the bottle, half empty, and the glass beside it. 'Yes,' he admitted, 'I've been trying to console myself.'

'Console yourself?' Susan sounded mystified.

'Yes.' There was a slight sob in his voice.

Thinking it through, Barry had decided that the best way to play this would be to appeal to Susan's considerable ego. If he could convince her that he would be devastated by losing her, but was nevertheless willing to forgo his own happiness for the sake of her own, surely that would secure his freedom.

'I know you're having an affair,' he blurted out.

'Barry,' she warned, 'remember the traffic—'

'I know, Susan. I followed you . . . saw you and . . . and Simon in the Co-Op car-park.'

There were now three images of her, and Barry wasn't quite sure which was the real one.

'You've been spying on me. Who gave you the—'

'We are married,' he reasoned.

'That doesn't give you the right to invade my privacy. And besides, it's not what you think.'

'But I saw you in the back of his car. You were on top of him.'

'Don't be so vulgar,' Susan shouted. 'Simon's insecure. He just needed to know that I really do like him, and I'm not just being kind because I feel sorry about his moles.'

'Oh, that's all right then . . . thank God . . . you're only dropping your knickers—'

'Christ, you're so base, Barry,' Susan said with loathing.

Barry realised it was all going terribly wrong. 'Look, all I'm saying is, I don't know how I'm going to cope with this . . .' He toyed with the empty glass. ' . . . but I'm not going to stand in your way.'

Susan's mouth dropped open and Barry pushed his advantage.

'When I saw the two of you on that stage, you reminded me of . . . of Clark Gable and Vivien Leigh.'

'We did?' Susan sounded interested. 'Si always says I remind him of Ingrid Bergman. He says the similarity in profile, especially, is uncanny.'

'Really? Look, what I'm saying . . . ' Barry went on, almost pleading now, 'is that when I saw you on that stage, I thought, who am I to stand in the way of two people with such an obvious rapport . . . a perfect merging of minds, talents . . . and bodies?'

Barry began to wonder whether he might possess some degree of acting talent himself.

Susan reached across and tenderly touched his hand, a stage tear trickling down her cheek.

'Who indeed?' she said softly. 'I've misjudged you, Barry. I'm so sorry.'

Barry let his head fall forward as if in grief, even though this made the room spin and brought on a feeling of sickness.

'I don't know what I'm going to do,' he moaned, 'but I'll let you have half the house, half the furniture, half the car . . . and then I'll just get out of your life.' He bit on his lip and his voice cracked as he said, 'I think the lines that will always bring some consolation are: 'Tis far better to have loved and lost, than never to have . . .'

Barry's voice trailed off as he caught sight of the furious look on Susan's face.

'What the hell are you talking about?' she screamed. 'If you think I'm going to give you half of everything I've worked and slaved for, just because you're not emotionally mature enough to cope with my having an affair, then you must be mad.'

'But Susan—'

'Don't you dare "But Susan" me – you monster.' She was livid. 'If my mother knew what you were putting me through . . .'

She stood up and ran from the room. Barry could hear her steps pounding on the stairs.

And it was at that moment he decided to kill her.

*

Barry had plenty of time in which to plan how he would do it, for it seemed that Simon Shafton had taken a penthouse flat – actually, it was two rooms over a fruit and vegetable shop, but theatrical folk will colour the facts with a thick veneer of grandeur – and Susan was helping with the decorating.

Barry took to reading a lot of crime fiction which proved invaluable in many ways.

Firstly, it seemed that the murderer, however clever, always made some small mistake which was picked up by the detective in charge, who invariably either loved opera or poetry, or had a drink problem.

Secondly, in domestic murders, as they're called, the victim's spouse always comes under close scrutiny. So that meant Barry would have to terminate his sweet arrangement with the comely Carrie, for he did not want the police digging up his personal life.

In any case Carrie – who definitely seemed to be lurching towards alcoholism – was proving to be an expensive diversion.

He told the unfortunate girl one Monday morning while they were checking that she had enough boxes of washing powder to last the day.

'Carrie,' he began solemnly, 'over the last few weeks you've come to mean a lot to me – probably more than you'll ever know. I just want you to believe that it's for your own good but . . . I'm not going to see you again . . .'

He paused, allowing her time to react; she didn't so he said, 'It's far better that we make a clean break. You'll thank me for it in years to come.'

Carrie nodded rather blankly, and Barry was sure that her bloodshot eyes had misted over. Anyway, somehow she managed to get through the day as if nothing had happened.

Barry knew that she had only agreed to go out with Ted, the fork-lift driver, to keep up the pretence. What a brave kid!

He would never let on that he knew though; she must deal with it in her own way. Time would heal the wounds.

The money he saved on rum and peppermint came in very handy for buying the aspirin.

He had reached the conclusion that, if he was to have any chance of getting away with it, he must make it look like an accident or suicide.

Exploring the possibilities with aspirins, he soon ran into problems. Not one of the crime books included guidelines on the amount of aspirins needed to bring about death, so he studied the suggested dosage instructions on the bottle and reasoned that these would veer towards the safe side.

He emptied the tablets from the bottle, divided them into four, added a few more to allow for a margin of error, and came up with a rough total of one hundred.

But after conducting numerous experiments, Barry finally had to concede that it was impossible to conceal the taste of one hundred aspirins in wine, mineral water, or tea.

Of course he could hit Susan on the head and render her unconscious, then pour the tablets down her throat, but he was forced to dismiss this method after reading *A Disorderly Death* by Tony Dolain.

In that book, Inspector Pitman – a man who spent his off-duty hours analysing the lyrics of Bob Dylan songs –

had caught his murderer by proving beyond any reasonable doubt that there was one wound on the back of the victim's head which could not have been sustained during her fall from the flat felt roof of her kitchen extension.

Pitman then knew that she must have been knocked out and hurled off the said roof, so he arrested the victim's husband. Barry shuddered when he read that, for it seemed that nothing was beyond the powers of technology now available to the police.

Pitman proved his case by sifting through rubbish at the local tip until he found a whisky bottle – of the brand the husband was known to drink – adhered to which were two hairs from the dead woman's head.

Although Barry did not think there was anyone at his local police station intelligent enough to decipher Bob Dylan's lyrics, he decided that this new-found information urged caution.

For a time he thought he had the perfect solution: he could push Susan down the stairs and then, as she lay senseless in the hall, shovel the tablets down her throat.

Then he read that if – in possible suicides – the police did not find a note, they tended to regard it as homicide. These detectives all seemed to be fiercely clever and decided such things by something called 'gut instinct'.

Then of course there would be the added complication of explaining why a woman who had taken a lethal overdose should suddenly drag herself from the bed, get dressed, walk out of the bedroom and throw herself down a flight of stairs.

Nevertheless, from that idea came the solution. It was perfect in every way; all he needed to do was make sure that no one saw him carry out the murder.

Then a near disaster occurred: Susan's attitude towards him changed. She became almost conciliatory; encouraged him to smoke in the house; even bought bottles of Scotch for him now and again.

She also took to meeting him in the hall when he came home from work, and lighting his cigarette for him.

One evening, after blowing out the match, she said, 'I know what you're going through, Barry – believe me, I know, but it's far worse for me.'

'Is it?' Barry asked dumbly.

'God, it is.'

She stalked off into the lounge. Barry followed and found her staring out of the window.

'I just want you to know that what's happening between Simon and me is nothing to do with us.'

Barry found that hard to follow.

'Oh no, Barry, no, no, no . . . and no, again,' she proclaimed. 'Whatever happens you'll always have my heart.'

'Yes, but he's getting the interesting bit,' Barry replied with candour.

'Is that what you want, Barry?' She strode towards him dramatically. 'Then take it. Push me down to the floor and take it. I'll do anything you want – no matter how obscene. You only have to ask.'

Barry wondered if she would take a hundred aspirin tablets if he told her they were aphrodisiacs. He could take a few first himself. But he quickly dismissed the idea; he knew from his reading that the police could always establish when the victim had last had sexual intercourse.

Would he be able to explain to the satisfaction of the

police why, in the middle of the sex act, his wife had suddenly decided to commit suicide, and why he had not taken steps to avert the tragedy? Even if he could, would the resulting publicity be beneficial to his image or chances of future relationships?

Back to Susan. She was saying, 'No . . .' quite meaningfully. ' . . . you're too sensitive to take me while another man is violating me. Just help me through this, Barry. I promise, in the next week, you'll find peace.'

He knew he would, but not in the way Susan meant.

His chance, when it came, was out of the blue, and at first he didn't realise it had arrived.

He was trudging up Crash Hill in total darkness, on his way home from work. For several weeks now Susan had been taking the car, leaving him to walk the four miles to and from the factory.

He saw a parked car when he was still some distance away from it and did not recognise it as his own until he drew level.

'Barry,' Susan called from the open window, 'get in. I want to talk to you.'

He climbed into the passenger seat. 'What is it, Susan?'

'I've reached a decision. I'm going to see Simon and tell him I want nothing more to do with him.'

'Are you sure that's wise?' Barry counselled earnestly.

'Yes, Barry, I know now where my future lies. But I'm frightened. He's a violent man . . . an ex-boxer. I've seen him tear telephone directories in half.'

Barry liked the sound of this; if Shafton was that violent, he might kill Susan himself. No, he chided himself, that was leaving too much to chance.

'That's why I waited here for you. I know what you're

like, you'll want to come and tell him that if he ever comes near me again, you'll thrash him to within an inch of his life . . .'

Barry gulped.

' . . . but I don't want you to, Barry, just understand that. Promise not to follow me.'

'Well, if you'd rather go on your own, that's fine by me.'

Then like a flash, it hit him . . . this was his chance! For so long he had pondered how to get Susan to this very place after dark.

'Thank you for that, Barry,' she said intensely. 'Now, for God's sake just kiss me like you really mean it . . . and let me be gone.'

Barry felt slightly sick as her lips fused to his.

In her passion Susan did not hear the click of her seat-belt as it was released. She thought nothing of his hand stealing round to the back of her neck.

As the embrace ended, they parted, and Barry smashed her head as hard as he could against the windscreen. Relishing the thud it made, he did it again before regaining control of himself.

Forcing himself to stop shaking Barry quickly climbed out of the car, and after checking that no one could see him, he ran up the embankment.

Minutes later he returned with two large bricks which he placed under the front wheels. Then getting back into the car he placed Susan's limp foot on the clutch pedal and put the gear shift into fourth.

He got out again and skirted round to the driver's side, said a quiet prayer, then reached through the open window and turned the ignition key.

The engine spluttered into life and Barry let out a

huge sigh of relief.

If he had guessed right, then Susan's foot should keep the clutch pedal depressed just long enough for the car to gather speed down the sharp decline. So when the police investigated the crash, the only conclusion they could reach would be that Susan had been driving down the hill, without her seat belt, when she lost control of the car.

He switched the dipped headlights on, removed the bricks, and held his breath, expecting the engine to stall at any moment. But no, the car began to roll and gather speed; then it shuddered and jolted as Susan's foot came free of the clutch.

He exhaled with relief as, with smoke trailing from its exhaust, the car careered on down the hill.

Barry carried on walking home, trying to act naturally. If any of the neighbours were watching they would have seen Susan go out earlier and Barry returning at his usual time. There would be nothing to connect the two events.

He had just committed the perfect murder. He had done it.

Now he must prepare to look suitably grief-stricken when the police called.

Inside the house he placed his Tupperware sandwich container on the hall table, took a cigarette from the packet and laughed.

Just as his thumb worked the lighter, Barry smelt gas. He neither saw nor felt the explosion, for he was part of it.

Two streets away, Simon Shafton was fingering his

moles when the explosion occurred.

The sound pleased him. He knew his idea had impressed Susan but one could never be sure that it would work as planned.

Susan had left the gas taps on at the cooker and left the house. The master stroke had been for her to meet that cretin, Barry, on the hill; that way he wouldn't wonder where she was when he got home . . . and he would light his cigarette as usual.

What could the police prove? A gas tap had been left on accidentally, that was all.

Now they could claim the insurance – not only for the house but also for Barry's life. Now they could be together.

He did love Susan deeply, but had doubted his feelings when, at first, she had suggested divorcing Barry and giving him half the house etcetera.

Simon set off for his rendezvous with Susan.

He was puzzled by all of the flashing blue lights he could see at the bottom of Crash Hill.

There seemed to be a fire of sorts. He could not be sure from this distance . . . but it looked like a car.

Reconstruction

James Hamilton-Paterson

Reconstruction

Well here I am folks it's me Tina walking down the High Street at coming up to News time on a Thursday evening followed by about three dozen cops. And that's just for starters. I'm also trying to walk like Karen plus I'm wearing all her clothes except her underwear. It's creepy enough anyway wearing the clothes of someone who's only been dead a week and the way this Pamela goes on or Woman Police Sergeant Buttrace or whatever she is she'd've had me wearing Karen's knickers. 'It's got to be as realistic as we can possibly make it, Tina,' she kept saying and yes here I am being as bloody realistic as they can possibly make me.

Specially the hair. Of course ever since the Quiz I've worn mine short only Karen still had hers long – blondes do that don't they, they're so proud of it they can't wear it long enough. 'Sweet-Faced Little Schoolgirl Karen' the newspapers call her. Yes well we at Bishop Trilby Comprehensive knew a different Karen didn't we? Anyway they fitted me up with a wig and I suppose in the dark with this sort of wobbly tart's walk on a pair of her poncy white heels I probably do look a bit like her, family resemblance and all that. Horrible thought. But what I'm really still wondering about's this wig. How did they get it? Do you reckon they've got dressing-up gear ready at every police station in the country? Just for identity parades and reconstructions of crimes? A funny idea, right, a cupboard in every station stocked up with stuff for everyone from kids to pensioners. 'Bit too clean-looking is he Mum for your boy? Got just the thing here, spray-on zits. They dry red with the little whitey-green bit on top like the real thing. Hold still son.'

That's made me laugh a bit and it's supposed to be wow! so serious all this. Anyway here we are at the traffic lights which Karen wouldn't have waited for in a month of Sundays but I stop at the pedestrian crossing like a good little girl. And here comes WPS Buttrace.

'Can you hold it a sec, love?' she says. 'We've got an old couple over there outside the newsagent's say you're ringing a bell. You've still got another thirteen minutes to the bridge.'

'That's easy Miss,' I say.

'I know. But the Tesco manager's sure about the time Karen left and you're just as sure about when you saw her pulled into the car on the other side of the bridge so she must've dawdled a bit on the way. Window-shopping probably. You feeling all right?'

'Yes Miss.' I put on my brave smile.

'Soon be over love. You couldn't be doing a better service for your cousin. She'll be really proud of you.'

'Do you really think she's still. . .?' Oh that catch in my voice. That's serious acting.

'We're all certain she's alive.' WPS Buttrace couldn't act her way out of a paper bag. 'Anyway she'd be proud of you doing this.'

Karen? Would she heck as like, she'd be hopping mad. Apart from the *main* reason of course she'd be pissed off about me wearing her clothes, specially the shoes. Karen wouldn't've ever lent me her shoes. She wouldn't've ever lent me anything except perhaps a dog with rabies. But here's Ms Fuzz talking into her radio. Pretty obvious what she is even though she's wearing ordinary clothes and now she's saying off you go again and don't forget we're just behind you. No, too right I shan't forget that.

So off we start and though I suppose I do look pretty much like any fourteen-year-old schoolgirl going home for tea after doing a couple of hours on the check-out I still think everyone's staring at me. They're not really and they'd better not because if they do they're going to get about three tons of Old Bill down their collars and it's off to the station for a good duffing-up. Feelings are running high around these parts as the local paper goes on pointing out every evening as if it's worried they'll stop running high and folks'll just go back to their tellies and remember Karen for a month as Sweet-Faced Little Schoolgirl Whatsername who some nutter bundled into a car one dark night and was never seen again.

In a way that'd be right though. It's not real is it? It's all too much like that old poof in that series about was it forensics or police pathology, you know, Quincy in America. Each week a new bod on the slab with the gutters all round it and those lumps under sheets coming out on sliding drawer things like filing cabinets. It's a good series though, you can learn a lot. There was this fellow shot someone with an icicle loaded in an air rifle. Dead neat. There's no bullet, not for long anyway, no exit wound and no trace of any . . . hey there's someone staring. God it's Philip Stott. Stott The Snot. Just for a bit the poor twit thinks I'm Karen of course and he's just about to come up and make her an offer she could never refuse but I certainly can thanks very much. Ha now he's done a doubletake and he knows it's me and he's put his hand to his mouth and gone off. Laughing probably. Or hiding those teeth of his. Wait till I tell Tracy tomorrow she'll die.

It makes you think how much your looks really count. I mean if it'd been poor Trace instead of Karen nobody would've called her Sweet-Faced. She's this really sweet person but she's honestly not a raving beauty. Funny though about Karen, you really noticed it how everyone specially the police and press who're after all supposed to want to find out The Truth ha-ha, all they wanted was to build Karen up into a sort of ace angel. Mind you when I was interviewed I admit I didn't come right out and say I thought my cousin was the pits and we fought like cats. But in the beginning when I was maybe a bit cool and offhand about her the interviewers would say something like 'I'm sure you don't really mean that Tina' and 'It's the shock talking' or 'You wouldn't want her to hear you've said that about her, would you?' And I wanted to say 'Couldn't care less, we've been saying much worse to each other's face for years.'

But anyway they aren't going to find her are they? So

sometimes after those interviews I just wanted to go up to the top of the clock tower on the Town Hall and yell as loud as I can 'Karen Cuddy's dead you dumb sods! And she didn't have a sweet face she had a tart's face! And if you think she was a little angel just ask around the boys at Bishop Trilby's! Fact!'

But of course I didn't do any of that. After a bit of trying to be truthful it was just easier to sort of go along with what they wanted to hear. They didn't care about motives or anything like that because they'd already made up their minds what'd happened. They wanted another innocent child victim of the Devon Beast? Fine, they got one. They got it right from the mouth of Karen's own cousin and practically next-door neighbour, quiet serious dark-haired Tina Murtree the promising scholar who recently represented Bishop Trilby's in *Round Britain Quiz* and was the last person to see her. That's me folks, the Girl whose Act of Courage will Help Police Trace her Cousin and Best Friend. Best friend that's a laugh.

Really there ought to be someone you can tell the truth to but not Mum of course and not Dad in a million years not with things as they are now. But it'd be great to be able to. I've got this really strong feeling I'd like to be able to say how it was between us, me and Karen I mean, and how I really am and how she really was. Tracy doesn't know the whole thing but she knows lots already and maybe I'll tell her one day. It's not like confessing or anything because it's not guilt honestly but like they say on TV 'setting the record straight'. What I can't stand is people just believing what the reporters write, sort of the official version and it's that version everyone always remembers. Obviously Karen can't've been the worst person who ever lived what with Hitler and that but she definitely wasn't like they pretend. So how could what happened to her be like they say it was? They always have to turn everyone into Angels or Monsters, have you noticed? Karen was a tart right enough but I must admit she wasn't stupid and frankly she nearly took my place on *Round Britain Quiz*. It doesn't make sense I mean she can't have known anything, I swear she never opened a book in her life she was far too busy with boys. And this Devon Beast bloke they've been after for over a year now I bet he's probably an ordinary married man sort of fatherly with glasses who just gets a bit carried away when flirts like Karen try it on and serve them right.

Anyway all I really want to tell someone is how she fancied herself rotten and didn't care who knew or whose boyfriend she went with, I mean you know what boys are they just can't help themselves not once they've had great cow eyes made at them and got all slurped over and petted. Now I think about it I don't know why Shiv and Elly and the others but specially Elly were so nice about how she treated them though Elly did get Dominic back in the end even if he was a bit different by then but anyway . . . Christ, nearly got run over! *That*'d look good in the papers: Missing Schoolgirl's Best Friend Killed While Helping Police. Here comes Ms Fuzz again.

'Tina dear do you want to stop?' she asks and puts her arm round me. 'You sure you're not getting too upset?'

'I'm all right Miss.' I put on my brave smile again, it's a goody.

'You were walking along in a daze.' Really she

oughtn't to be talking to me since she didn't to Karen last Thursday. I guess Ms Fuzz remembers too because she gives my arm another quick squeeze and drops behind.

Be honest I can't understand the point of this whole caper. I mean it's stupid. The cops say it's suppose to jog someone's memory who might've been here this time last week and perhaps saw Karen being followed slowly by the bloke in the car. That's their theory anyway that she was kerb-crawled somewhere between leaving Tesco's and halfway along Mitchells Lane. But I don't see how they can learn much more than I've already told them. What I said was I was coming back from the library, perfectly true, and by chance I came out into Mitchells about fifty metres behind Karen. Okay it's pretty dark there but I knew it was her because I see her every day of my life worse luck and anyway she only lives four doors down. But how can you be positive? they asked. 'Well who else besides her from round here's gone missing at tea time in the last two days?' I said and you could see that skinny WPC longing to have a go at me for giving them lip but she couldn't, not with me being the Tragic Witness and Mum and Dad being there and all.

So from where Mitchells Lane starts there's no point doing this reconstruction thing because there wasn't anyone else about, just me and her. There never is much because there's only the back of Scumbag Seddon's farm then the railway then another bit and Farm Close where we live. One bus every year about. But from Tesco's to Mitchells Lane is just as pointless if you ask me because nobody knows what route she took. She might've gone round the corner to Boots for some of that hair toner she used to get through by the gallon, ought've got a bulk discount. That would explain why she took quite long to get to the bridge. But they decided she went straight along the High Street like I've just done so here we are at the War Memorial and about to leave all the lights and people and turn up towards the station for a bit before we head off down Mitchells into the Great Black Unknown like in *Star Trek*. And only I know how pointless it all is except I've been wondering if they don't think so too but feel they've just got to go along with it. Sort of tradition really. So here we are.

And now we're actually in Mitchells Lane and there's only one street lamp every hundred metres about, those mauvey things. I wish they were that orangey kind which do funny things to make-up and nail varnish, those always seem a bit cosier. And here's where I told them I first spotted Karen up ahead level with those creepy old cowsheds Seddon's abandoned, he must be the laziest farmer for miles. And to be honest I don't want to go on with this, it's like having your head forced down a sack further and further. There's nobody else around, wasn't last Thursday either so what's the use me walking along a lane in the dark dressed as someone else? Those old shed things are getting to me. You really feel you're on your own down Mitchells.

I've just had a funny thought. What if this Beast bloke really is waiting *right now* parked just over the other side of the bridge? And as I walk past his car a door opens and he lunges out and grabs me and drives off? Right in front of WPS Buttrace and her merry men who he doesn't see it being so dark and them so far behind? That would actually be a bit of a giggle but perhaps not for me. Imagine the newspapers on *that* one . . . Of course they'd secretly love it, they love to see the police with red faces. That's what they're best at, journalists, pointing fingers and getting all pompous. They don't actually *do* anything do they? That's how you know for sure Superman doesn't exist because so few crimes get solved. You can't imagine that wimp who interviewed me asking such silly questions if he'd really been mild-mannered Clark Kent. *He* wouldn't want to've known about how good Karen was at basketball or where she went to discos. He'd've been off zipping up his cape in the phone box and inside an hour there'd be the poor old Devon Beast done up like a parcel in Xantrium web and dumped on the Chief Constable's desk. Christ we're passing the place right now and I hate this and it's spookier than I ever thought and oh Dad, Dad please why can't I tell you? But I can't.

And why can't I, you *stupid* man? Because I've gone and got her off your back for you that's why, the cow. Did you honestly think your own daughter wouldn't notice? All those Saturdays working on that smelly car out in the garage and her just happening to come by with sandwiches from your own sister as if our Mum couldn't make them? Her leaning over that boring old engine like a boy and pretending to sound interested with her boobs showing down the front of that blouse of hers? I reckon after a bit even you could've seen she was trying it on but that didn't stop you doing your Uncle Terry act and taking her down the coast that day everyone else had the flu and it was as much as we could do to drag ourselves as far as the kitchen to make hot lemon let alone ponce off to Bideford.

Poor Dad. Sometimes I get really angry, know why?

Because you still think I'm innocent little Tina, Tina the Scholarship Girl who's always got her nose in a book and's been on a nationwide quiz and who's too innocent to know what half that stuff in Quincy means. You and Mum were dead against me doing this walk lark weren't you? I mean you could see the cops were really keen but they didn't dare go on about it and when I actually agreed to do it you nearly had a fit. It's not your fault. It's that generation stuff when the one thing you can't tell about kids is how much they *know*. Kids're different now from when you were young. Of course you're young really not even forty yet and you don't look it but things've changed. You look at me and I know you're seeing Tina Teacher's Pet who's going to university. But I can tell you I'm Tina with Teeth. Else how could your little innocent daughter've thought it out, just brilliant, how to get you out of trouble, probably keep you out of *prison* if the plods found out about you and Karen. Tart she might've been but she was still underage by about three years. But me making sure they thought of the Devon Beast like that, not bad eh? The perfect suspect and alibi. But of course you aren't going to know, no one is.

Okay we're past the worst bit and the bridge is coming up about thirty metres away with its one light and this is getting really silly. A couple of cars have passed and one of them was Douglas from up the end of the Close but they'll have talked to him already since he's a regular commuter. They'll've got his number again though I bet. It's all so unreal this and not happening to me at all, just like a film. Back there I expected to feel really bad or see Karen standing on the verge all dripping with sump oil and grinning and beckoning slowly like in *Cindy* or was it I don't know, the other one where this fellow gets pulled towards where he's hidden the body like it was magnetic. But it wasn't like that at all, just really scary for a moment because of something you know and nobody else in the whole world knows. It can't have been too awful though can it as I was thinking more about Dad than about her deep under that old tractor oil. Which reminds me that Tina with Teeth also has Terrible Hands and for some reason having that thought *is* scary. Perhaps in a quiz some day you know many years later they'll ask 'Which schoolgirl had Terrible Hands?'

'Tina!' Christ she makes me jump stupid witch and here they all are the Old Gang. They've caught up, them and their alsatians and radios and stuff and in the dark who's to know if they're goodies or baddies? 'It's okay now love,' she's saying. 'That's it.'

We're in the middle of the bridge and up along the railway line to the left you can see the lights of the station.

'And that's where it happened,' says a copper and they all shine their torches up the road and I'm just about to say Oh no it wasn't when I remember in time. Got to stick to my story. They're all staring at the spot as if they're expecting an action replay, you know at the same place and the same time the little drama I invented for them'll happen again like something not yet finished properly. We all walk towards the scene of the imaginary crime which has already been crawled over by the forensic guys until they were dusting the dandelions at the roadside for prints. As we get there the Buttrace does her arm-squeezing number again and

I do wish she wouldn't because it makes me feel fakey like when you skive off school with a pretend illness and have to listen to people being sympathetic. Still here comes Tina the Actress with her brave little shudder.

'We're all very grateful you know Miss,' says this manly voice in the dark. 'It takes courage to re-enact a terrifying incident. We all give you full marks.'

It's a quiz after all. 'Do you think it was useful?' I ask not quite certain of my voice.

'Oh no question Miss. Very useful indeed. Several good leads which we're getting on to right away.' Lying sod. 'We don't want to raise your hopes falsely about your cousin of course but we now think there's a real chance of finding poor Karen alive. This fellow's pulled the same caper so many times now we think he's done it once too often. We'll get him, don't you worry. You're perfectly safe. We'll be looking after you until he's in custody.' Oh great.

And so on and on. And because they don't want to know what it was all really about they'll go on believing Tina the Tragic Witness so they won't bother to search off the road anywhere before that place I said I saw her being pulled into the car. One day of course someone'll dig out that old well for something . . . But by then the wretched Beast'll be doing life and they'll just lumber him with one more body which'll all neatly fit in with the time and place of his famous Rampage (the papers of course) and his equally well-known habit of strangling with hair ribbon.

And I'm scared shitless to tell the truth but it's done now and it's like a weight off my life. Specially when here we all are walking up my own garden path and I can see Mum ironing in front of the telly just like we were carol singers or something and I think it's because everyone's play-acting really and even I forget I'm still dressed as Karen and obviously Dad who opens the door has completely forgotten and for an awful moment I catch that look in his eye before he remembers and pulls himself together. But I've seen and it's not a look a daughter forgets and at that moment I *know* I'm right, that the whole thing really is a weight off all our lives.

War Crime

Bill James

War Crime

You'll be thinking, this is no place for an elderly woman, day in day out, haunting a building site, gaping at mechanical diggers. I'm certainly not interested in one of the 'six-bedroom prestige homes' they'll erect. I live alone now.

This was a Second World War Royal Air Force airfield at the edge of the town, abandoned years ago. Now, in 1993, they are breaking up the runways, ready for one of those 'executive' estates, and as a matter of fact I'm here to see whether a boy called Peter Milton is found under the concrete. He will be wearing a wedding ring.

I call him a boy and this is how I still think of dear, vile Peter. He was a boy when his life ended in 1943 and I put his beautiful body in the ground. They were just constructing this airfield. I was seventeen and Peter fourteen. At the time it seemed a mighty barrier, this difference in age – woman, child. Now, of course, the gap between him and me would be nothing. Perhaps I was wrong to worry about it even then. The thought harrows me. So do many others from those damned, imperishable days.

He was not local, but evacuated here from London to escape German bombing. Although by 1943 the blitz had slackened and many evacuees went back, Peter and a few others stayed. I was working in council Welfare, my first job after leaving school. While I began as just an office-girl, senior staff were scarce in the war and soon I had to help with liaison – making sure the evacuees were happy. Peter and I were bound to have a lot of personal contact. Absolutely nothing untoward about this, believe me.

These Londoners seemed more grown up than children raised here – sharper and tougher, girls as well as boys. What you would expect: big city against small town. I was still at school myself when they first arrived just after war was declared in September 1939, and some of the girls were put in my class. They knew so much: not about school work, but other topics, grown-up topics, and Peter was the same, although only ten years old then. If he and his friends met you in the street they would sometimes shout crude, shocking, terribly intimate things.

When I came to know him better, I discovered he was not really like that. He could be sensitive, he had feelings. If not, he might still be alive and I would not need to wait near this disturbed ground every day, scrutinising dirt. The workmen are puzzled.

Peter disappeared near the middle of that year, 1943. At first, nobody bothered. People said he had run away, back to London. Occasionally, evacuees did that. He never arrived there, though, and eventually police here began a search. Peter and his friends used to play in sand-dunes on the beach, making dens, fighting battles, boiling crabs, and this was where police, troops and volunteers concentrated their efforts, in case he had been buried by a fall. Finally, they dug out a place Peter had made with bits of drift-wood and a sheet of corrugated iron. They did not find him, but some of his things were there: a Mickey Mouse alarm clock, army badges which he collected, and his autograph book. Very unfortunately, I had put my signature in that, and a line from a quite famous poem, 'Gather ye rosebuds while ye may'. The poem concerns girls, really, but it had seemed right for him when I wrote it. I told the police I had no idea where he might be, and it was absolutely true, then. They asked what the poetry meant and I replied at once that it was only to fill up the page and came from another time, indeed, another century. Again, true.

It had been one of our good days when I wrote that. Peter could be so delightful, and he could be an utterly evil swine, with true London swinishness. When we had good days, I would take him on outings, such as watching military parades to celebrate 'Warships Week' or 'National Savings Week' or 'Tanks Week', displays meant to prop civilian morale. Sometimes we would go to the cinema, or to historical places like the cottages used by political agitators called Chartists for meetings last century, or we might gather wild flowers or blackberries in the country. This was simply part of my work and perfectly normal, believe me. You see, it was partly because we gathered wild flowers together that I wrote what I did.

His mother sent him the book from London for his fourteenth birthday and he said I must be the first to sign, because I mattered most. This was silly but very sweet. That's what I meant – he could be really considerate. On these nice days he would talk to me as if I were his girl friend, and he would try to use his hands and so on in the pictures or when we were blackberrying. Naturally, I had to stop that. He was too young. This is what I meant before: they were so grown up, these London kids. I don't know what went on between him and some evacuee girls, especially one called Joy. That used to make me horribly miserable and angry, though I never let him see I cared. It would not have been proper. In some ways, Peter was a right little shit. (That kind of language, I would not have used then, of course. Women and girls didn't. But this is 1993 and things have changed, for better or worse I don't know. In any case, I and the rest of us in the town learned quite a bit from those evacuees, including some coarseness, I'm afraid.) There were bound to be times when I felt overwhelming hate for Peter, weren't there? At those moments it was as if I ceased to be myself and an appalling rage took over. It would always fade, but not always in time.

When I wrote that poetry in his book, we were behind the Chartist cottages on an afternoon out there, and he wanted to kiss me, I mean, really kiss me, on the mouth, bodies close, but I would not allow that, either. I could not. I told him, I was like a sister or his school teacher. He replied that the poetry said something different – he could be so clever, that one – but I told him it was only poetry, from another, distant time. We had a laugh and he did not get at all vicious, not that day.

Then, just a week afterwards, he somehow found out

about an entirely separate matter, and suddenly he changed. Peter could be fond, he could be a ripe peril. You see, I had kept quiet about certain new aspects of my life: I was sure it would be exceptionally unwise to tell him I needed somebody more my own age. He would refuse to understand. So, in the street, he stood right in front of me and said at the top of his squeaky, wild voice, 'Some dirty ice-a-da-creamo Wop's sticking it up you, is he?'

I still feel ill when I recall those savage words. It was how they talked, the Londoners, even after years with us. And it was how they thought – vulgarity, aggression. You see, this was his sickening, glorious jealousy, which would lead to such a horrible end. I try never to think of it now, but the memories often force their way back. He had no damn rights over me. I was older, a woman, really. Good God, friends of my age were married and starting families.

The evacuees were not our only visitors at that time. Just outside the town stood a camp for Italian prisoners of war, who used to help the farmers. This was what Peter meant when he said 'Wop'. To be fair, everybody called Italians that then, and said all they could do was sell ice cream. These were the enemy, of course, like Jerries and Japs. But most of the Italians seemed gentle, not real soldiers. By this time, Italy was almost out of the war, anyway. The camp had very little security, and prisoners worked unguarded on the farms. This was how I met Carlo.

It happened first when I went gathering wild flowers by myself one day on my bike. Peter should have come but failed to turn up, so it was absolutely his own filthy fault. I felt sure he was with one of the girl evacuees:

Joy, I should think, the easy, scheming cow, giving joy to every boy she fancied, which meant most – I don't exaggerate. That really hurt me, but I decided not to look for him. Carlo was cutting a farm hedge near the patch of wild flowers. He could speak some English and was nice and funny and a bit dreamy, but not as beautiful as Peter. Carlo had quite a nose. The thing about Peter was his lovely long, soft, dark hair and brown eyes that could be so wonderfully warm. I was younger than Carlo, though only a few years, and I felt quite happy with him. He could often sneak out, and I began to go to see him, especially on Sunday afternoons, and he would tell me about Italy. He came from a place called Bolzano and said he had been a boot repairer there, but was studying while a prisoner and might become a teacher or even a headmaster.

One day, he said we would marry after the war, and, if they sent him away to another camp or back to Italy he would come and find me the moment he could. I was not sure, but later he gave me a gold ring that used to belong to his mother, who was dead. Naturally, I was careful and wore it only when I saw him. Usually, I kept it hidden on a cord around my neck. I knew people would think it bad for a girl to be with an Italian prisoner, a kind of betrayal of our troops and Mr Churchill, and I never showed the ring or told anyone about Carlo. How Peter discovered his existence, I still don't know. He had this stinking London slyness, those lovely, stinking, miss-nothing, brown eyes.

I think he began to watch me secretly. One Sunday afternoon, I was in some woods with Carlo, when he rolled away suddenly and sat up because he had heard a noise. Quickly, we began to dress. Then, out from the trees, rushed Peter and four other boys, all of them London friends of his. They had hammers and iron bars and began to beat Carlo before he could get to his feet and defend himself.

They struck him on the head and face and lower until he was unconscious. Peter hit him again and again, using some of that gross London language: 'See what we do to Wops who fuck our girls? And on a Sunday, too. He's not kitted, I see. Are you? You'll be hatching a little Musso bastard – thought of that? And where d'you get that fucking ring?' I did not answer but was so upset and enraged that I told Peter I never wanted to speak to him again. He laughed and said I would soon come crawling because I needed him so badly. But I meant it. That anger stayed with me quite a while, and I gave notice and left Welfare so I would not have to meet him.

That Sunday of the incident, I hurried to the camp and told Carlo's friends and they came to carry him back. He was unconscious. When I went on Monday to find how he was, a prisoner said Carlo died from head wounds the previous evening, without coming round. I never discovered if they even brought a doctor. During the war, it was another time, and Carlo only a prisoner. This was murder, of course, a horrible crime, but not one to interest the police much then. Troops killed Italians all the time in battle and nobody would worry much about another one dead. And, in any case, Carlo should not have been out of the camp. I knew the British commandant would want to keep it all quiet, or he might be in trouble. Probably he reported the death as due to a camp fight. And witnesses? I felt so sad but could never have publicly said the truth. People would think I was foully cheap to be like that with an Italian in the open air on what they termed the Sabbath. I never read anything of the killing in the local Press, nor even heard of a funeral.

Two months later Peter disappeared. I had seen him lurking near my parents' house, where I was living then, but avoided him by using back lanes. For a few days after the den was found, police and soldiers dug out more sand hills. They discovered nothing else. At the end, people said he must have gone swimming alone and drowned. I knew it was not true. Like all the London children, he hated the sea. I used to take him to the beach sometimes, but although he put his swimming trunks on he never went near the water. He had a quite tall, slim body, yet not weak-looking. In any case, it was nearly winter when he disappeared and the sea would be too cold.

As a matter of fact, detectives came to see me four times about the autograph book, and kept on and on with their questions, but I still said the piece of poetry meant nothing special. And, perhaps, really, it didn't in the end. I wouldn't let it, couldn't let it. But, naturally, all their damn nosiness made me think back to that splendid day when we went to the Chartist cottages and, on a Sunday afternoon, one week after the search for Peter was finally abandoned, I cycled there. What I needed then was something to bring comfort through joyous memories of him. In winter the cottages would not be open to visitors, but that did not matter.

Arriving, I went around the back where I had written in the autograph book. That quotation had just come to me out of nowhere, and, despite all the suspicion from police, I never regretted it. There was little I could regret in my contacts with Peter. What I regretted above all, and still grieve over, was the way I had broken those contacts, the way I had turned away from him in my fury after the serious banging he gave Carlo.

For a few moments, recollections of that happy day with the autograph book did rush back when I saw the cottages again. I felt pleased I had come. Sometimes a special location can create that sort of marvellous thrill, though it's all rubbish, of course: a place is only a place. Then, while I was still rejoicing at my decision, I found a window at the rear had been broken. That troubled me, but I did not know why. After a moment, I put my hand through and unfastened the catch. For a couple of minutes, I remained outside, no longer feeling joyful, yet knowing I must enter. Peter and I had gone inside last time, and this wish now was part of that deep urge to re-live all the previous visit. I climbed in.

There was a strange smell, which I did not remember from before. The window led into a little larder, with dim-wit models of a nineteenth-century cabbage and loaf on the shelf, to show that in those days, too, people used to eat, and it was when I opened the door from this larder into the single downstairs room that I saw Peter.

I can think about this now and stay calm, but for years after that day, I was unable to speak of it. Thank God, there was no call to speak of it. In fact, everything demanded silence. Some agonies are private.

To make visitors think they were having a real trip back in time, the council had kept these cottages as they were in history, and Peter Milton had hanged himself by the neck with rope fixed on a ceiling hook, once used for bacon sides too big for the larder. These hooks had to be strong because you did not want a great meat slab smashing down on one of the plentiful Victorian kiddies in its crib. There were some old chairs and other ancient furniture in the cottages and he had stood on a chair and kicked it away. It lay on its side now against the wall. He had brought the rope here, sure of what he intended. And he must have walked all that distance: I saw no bike outside. It all showed real determination, a real plan, and raw, unspeakable torment.

Of course, he had been there quite a long time. For a while I did not know what to do and thought of climbing back out of the window and cycling away. I could achieve nothing here, put nothing right. A section of my mind said this was nobody I knew, not now – this was nobody at all, not any longer: in the past, yes, someone sparkling and fine, with, admittedly, certain duff character aspects, but those were part of his liveliness, even if they meant someone else's harsh death. Now, no character at all.

And then I decided I could not treat Peter like that: leave him dangling on a pig hook, perhaps until the holiday season started again with all its sunshine and chattering folk on happy outings. I owed him more. This boy had killed for me. In many ways that was monstrous, of course, but it seemed also rather binding, in its way. Looking at him dead, I had to think even more than that: he had killed twice for me, for me alone. I brought back the chair he had used himself and, standing on it, tried to push the knot in the rope up and over the point of the hook so he would fall. When he was down I might be able to manage something. But I could not move that knot. This was the only way I could see to get him free. Free? How could he be free? But I had no other word. Because of tautness, it was impossible to undo the knot. He had made an excellent job of that. I thought of him reaching up and taking care over it, jerking down a few times with his hand to test, so he knew there would be no mistake when it got his jolting though boyish weight.

I was working with my fingers above my head, which made things very difficult, and his body, spinning slowly now and then, pulled down on the rope so it resisted all my pushing up. I paused. Of course, I should have realised that a broken window meant bits of glass, and I could have found one and sawed the rope. My brain was not doing very well, though, that day. It was as if I felt I had to release him by my own strength and effort, and cutting the rope did not come into it, could not. This was something I needed to do for Peter, and it had to be difficult, a hard and worthwhile task for a dear, beloved crony. Standing on the chair, I had my face and head more or less level with his, and I knew that in a moment I would have to put my arms around his middle and try to lift him, easing the load off the rope while I attempted again to free him. In a grim way it was like the closeness of lovers, that merging into each other. How it always was with Peter and me: like lovers, only like.

If it were not for his clothes, he would have been difficult to recognise, what with the time he had been there and the quite noticeable disturbances throughout him that being hanged caused. I remember feeling war had taken me too fast into the adult world of ugliness and wise despair.

Bending my legs a little, I took hold of Peter around his waist, then tried to lift him and get the cruel tension off the rope. Peter's frame did not feel like a body, of course – so unyielding after the time he had been there. No, he could not be mistaken for a lover.

I managed to get a tiny bit of slack into the rope. Then, though, I had to free one hand, reach high again and strive to push the knot up and over the hook point. This meant that I would have to keep Peter's weight off by clutching him with one arm only. I rested there for a few seconds, still pressing him to me with both arms – a kind of afflicted, unwholesome, very late, farewell hug – then increased the pressure with my right arm and quickly raised my left hand to try to slide the knot up.

It did not work at once. I was gasping and my legs shook. Of course, I was not in the best condition for such a struggle and I feared I would have to release him before I had finished, or that I would topple from the chair. I needed help, and help was the last thing I wanted. Then, somehow, the knot did get over the hook's tip and the rope's end glanced against my shoulder as it tumbled. I think I laughed aloud at this little triumph. People must have giggled and had pleasure in this cottage when it was lived in, but probably nobody ever giggled in here before over getting a revered corpse unhung. I lowered Peter to the ground with as much control as I could – not very much. He hit the boards with two sharp, hard sounds. At first he landed on his feet and the noise came from his shoes. He actually stood upright briefly and for that second I could almost see him as he used to be, a cheerful, war-torn kid in a paisley pullover. His face was away from me then, so I did not have to look at the most telling aspects, and his shoulders and back of the neck and head could have been, just could have been, those of a living person.

Then, though, he tumbled to the side and struck the floor with a hard, heavy rap, the rope trailing from him like the lead of a break-away dog. I stepped down from the chair and went to him. Methodically, I searched his clothes. That seemed immensely necessary. There was not much, but in the pocket of his trousers a note in a folded envelope addressed to me with big capital letters, so there would be no mistake. It also said PRIVATE on the envelope in even bigger letters, which was thoughtful, but would have failed to keep other eyes out if I personally had not had the timeliness to find him. The note said: 'There will be no rosebuds for me to gather. You don't even talk to me any longer. Why should I wait?'

About this I had a cry, though nothing too long or too loud. Lately, I had learned ways to keep things in check. He was announcing, was he, that his life meant nothing if it did not include me, and I had shut him out through anger? He had been a child, but with the thoughts and hopes of a man.

Obviously, I burned that letter as soon as I reached home. It would be a memento of him now, but not at all the kind I want. This was a brutal accusation, and too bloody fair. I went to my room and then sneaked out of the house so my mother would not notice. I had found some old potato sacks in our shed and I took them in my saddle-bag when I cycled back to the cottages. With these sacks I made what I think could be regarded as a duly respectful covering and, wrapping Peter in it, set out to drag him to where the airfield was under construction. This seemed an awful thing to do with someone who had been so comely, bumping and tugging him over rough ground. It took hours, mostly across fields. Now and then I had to pause with him under a hedge through fatigue or because I heard people near. The sacks still smelled of potatoes. Fortunately, the black-out was in force then, and even when we came near houses light did not fall on us. No question, we were an unusual couple.

Men had left tools where they were constructing runways and I dug a small grave and carefully eased him in. I took the sacking off him first and burned that later at home, like the letter and the envelope. I knew it would be wrong to include such workaday stuff in his final spot. Before I covered his body with soil, I took the ring off the cord around my neck and put it on his marriage finger. That seemed absolutely right, and anyone would have done the same. I placed him face down. Always we think of people buried looking up, like seeking the light. I suppose it is a religious thing – the eyes sightless, yet directed towards salvation, heaven, God. I could not bear to think of the dirt falling in around his eyes and cheeks and nose, though. A week later they slapped on the concrete, thick enough for loaded bombers.

There are still these days when I cannot resist coming here, but I've no real hope now of seeing what's left of Peter or the ring again, though I will attend once or twice more while the machines are working near that notable area. You can see that the ring would have been a sweet reminder of both Peter and Carlo, not that I could care less about Carlo, with his dreary looks and endless, greasy talk about Italy, or Wopland as we used to call it in the war. He was going back to his drab work as a boot repairer, and all that business about making it to headmaster was sky pie. Thank God, he never could come looking for me after the war. It is Peter I think of all the time, and his brilliant, ownership anger on finding us undoubtedly conjoint in the woods, his marvellous eyes so injured and agleam.

Fortunately, even without the ring, I have something special and, yes, living, to remember him by. I am sure, unswervingly sure, that my son was conceived that day Peter killed the father. These are rare circumstances, I should think. I called my son Paolo, which I felt to be a happy combination of the two names, Peter and Carlo. I was quite lucky not to lose him through the contortions with Peter's corpse. By the time Paolo was born in 1944, Britain and Italy were at peace, so local folk would not be too bothered about an Italian name. I decided, sod what they thought, anyway. I don't consider it at all disrespectful to the dead to say Paolo grew up a lot better looking than his dad and luckily got my nose.

A Matter of Taste

Nancy Livingston

A Matter of Taste

The room was hot because Aunt Mildred preferred it like that but the heat released unwanted perfumes: eau de cologne from her lacy handkerchief, rose-scented furniture polish. Most heady of all were the bowls of pot-pourri that made Hugh feel dizzy. The mix was about right, though: a trace of femininity plus an obsession with cleanliness. That just about summed up Aunt Mildred.

As future inheritors of her wealth, he and Calum had been dragged here on duty visits since childhood. Hugh acknowledged he should by now be rejecting his aunt's hand-outs – she made him squirm every time she gave him a cheque. He was qualified, he shouldn't need extra money – the trouble was, he couldn't manage without it. God alone knew what would happen if she didn't fork out today . . . Sweat broke out, partly from the heat, mostly from remembering why he was here.

Besides, if he rejected her kindness, it would leave Calum free to work on her feelings and his brother was adept at that. Always her favourite nephew, Calum might persuade her to exclude Hugh altogether. It was bad enough listening to Aunt Mildred praise him – 'Calum should have been the doctor, not you, Hugh. All that charm and those good looks – lady patients would find his bedside manner irresistible.' Hugh gritted his teeth and tried to pretend he didn't care. At least Calum had the grace to look embarrassed.

He'd once attempted to copy Cal's charming lazy smile. It didn't work; Aunt Mildred accused him of pulling faces. Cal had the looks, charisma – why did no one realise how bone-idle he was? When he accused him of it, his brother simply laughed. 'You're the only one who's noticed, Hugh. I've managed to fool everyone else, including Aunt Milly.'

Hugh's expression reduced him to giggles. 'If looks could kill. . .! Cheer up. Some of us are born lucky, some have to work for a living – life just ain't fair.' Which didn't improve Hugh's feelings towards him.

Mildred's fortune was to be divided between them – but when? The waiting had become unendurable. Surely she couldn't last much longer? Her angina was worse. Hugh was too cautious to discuss her case with her GP but he'd read the label on the bottle and knew the strength of her pills.

She was watching him now, those penetrating blue eyes never missing a thing. Calum might make her laugh with his anecdotes but her attention was on Hugh.

'Lost a shilling and found sixpence?'

She'd caught him off balance. 'Not – necessarily.'

'It is money though, isn't it, I'm right about that? Why else would the pair of you turn up unannounced?' she sneered, provoking him deliberately. 'Calum never could manage on his grant but you Hugh, I cannot understand. A hospital doctor on a regular salary, it's disgraceful you should still be expecting money – try not to grind your heels in my carpet.'

Hugh kept a grip on his temper. He wanted to scream as Calum blundered in, attempting to put matters right. 'It's my fault, Aunt Milly. I need the cash, not Hugh. The bank manager sent one of his billets-doux last week, that's why I asked if I could tag along today.'

He beamed, confident he'd set the record straight. Hugh seethed. This visit had been planned with such care. When Calum asked for a lift, every instinct warned him against it. He'd only capitulated when he realised that as her favourite, Calum might put Mildred in a receptive frame of mind.

It was when they were in the car Calum revealed he was about to ask for money. It had been too late to turn back. There was nothing to be salvaged, Hugh would have to come back again on his own. Calum hadn't wasted any of his charm on Mildred today, he was already asking for two hundred pounds as the minimum sum to cover his needs. 'Apart from the cost of books, my bar bill last term was horrendous.'

That was idiotic! Despite his stupor, Hugh recognised it was the worst possible approach with Mildred.

'What makes you imagine I'm willing to subsidise your drinking habits?' she snorted. 'Is that right about you, Hugh? You don't need a sub? If so, it's the first time that's ever happened – wonders will never cease.' Hugh managed a sickly grin.

'I trust you're impressed, Aunt. As Cal said, we came to see how you were—'

'Rubbish! You're both praying for me to drop dead so you can get your hands on the lot – it's like entertaining a pair of vultures. Any minute I expect *you* to produce your stethoscope, to check whether I'm still alive. Well, I'm sorry to disappoint you both but I'm perfectly fit, and capable of leaving every penny to the Cats' Protection League.'

She wasn't as well as she claimed. Automatically, Hugh noted the signs: as her agitation increased so did the blue tinge round her mouth.

'Now, now, Aunt Mildred . . . ' Calum had finally realised all was not well and sounded anxious. 'Those dear moggies wouldn't appreciate such generosity whereas Hugh and I would be eternally grateful.'

Mildred looked at him speculatively. 'Were you being honest when you said two hundred pounds would be enough, or have you other financial problems?'

Don't fall into the trap, Hugh begged silently but Calum had plunged in. 'Quite frankly, a thousand quid would get me out of a hole. I had to swop my old banger last month. I know it's asking a lot but if we called it an advance against my trust money—'

'*Your* trust money!'

He pressed on blithely, 'Quite frankly, Aunt Milly, my old faithful wouldn't have passed its MOT—'

'Spare me the details.' Calum had opened his mouth. At her tone, he closed it again, quickly. Hugh felt suicidal; how long before he dare try and interest Mildred in his problems after this?

'Stupid, feckless . . . ' She was working herself into a state. 'Your silly mother spoiled the pair of you so it's up to me to teach you a lesson.' She took a couple of deep breaths to calm her fluttering heart. One more push, Hugh thought desperately; with her condition that's all it would need. As he heard her next words, the desire to throttle her was overwhelming.

'I've decided to make a new will,' she announced. 'Stuart is coming round this evening, to discuss it. The trust arrangements will be abolished. Instead, you'll each be given five thousand pounds – a nice round sum in my opinion – to clear any outstanding debts and enable you to start afresh. I intend bequeathing all the remaining capital, approximately five hundred thousand pounds, to War on Want.'

Hugh couldn't prevent what happened next. Mildred's housekeeper Frances, coming in with the tea tray, stood in shocked amazement as Calum exploded. Fists clenched, towering above his aunt, his handsome weak face was contorted with anger. Mildred was left in no doubt as to what he thought of her, of the tedious visits throughout their childhood, the bribes from their mother to persuade two sulky teenagers to do their duty every month.

In the silence that followed, Mildred murmured, 'Well, Hugh? Have you nothing to add? Calum apparently includes you in this!'

He ought to have denied everything and praised her past generosity, anything to soften the effect of Calum's words. Instead, at this most crucial moment of all, he was tongue-tied. Calum ordered, 'Come on. Let's get out of here.'

It was feeble but if he stayed, Mildred would accuse him of wanting to crawl. Leaving with Calum damned him. A quick glance at her face confirmed it. Putting aside thoughts of throttling her, he now wanted to murder Cal. What should have been a quest for cash to stave off disaster had turned into a catastrophe.

Back in the car Hugh found his voice and his attack was blistering. 'You bloody great cretin – you've done for us completely. Where in hell am I going to find three thousand quid?'

Calum was open-mouthed. 'Christ, Hugh! What kind of mess are you in?' His outburst of temper was fading fast. 'She'd never have forked out that much, ever.'

Hugh's mouth tightened. It had slipped out, he hadn't intended to tell Calum. 'Forget it.'

'Yes, but—'

'I said, forget it. Thanks to you, we've lost everything.'

Calum shrugged uneasily. 'She didn't really mean it about Stuart – she just said that to frighten us. Listen, Hugh, if you really do need that sort of money, Aunt Milly is your only hope.'

Hugh's fists were so tightly clenched, the nails bit into his palms; he wasn't a fool, he didn't have to be told that! 'The trouble with you, Cal, you still think you can charm your way out of a disaster. Mildred isn't stupid. She was perfectly serious and once that new will is signed and witnessed, we're done for.'

As swiftly as he'd lost his temper, Calum regained his senses. 'I'll apologise. Tomorrow I'll send her flowers. I'll go round and tell her she's wonderful, that kind of thing.'

It was so utterly futile, Hugh couldn't stifle the choke in his voice. 'What in God's name did you hope to achieve by shouting? We've put up with far worse – why lose your temper now?'

'Today was the last straw.' Calum was sulky. 'Have you ever worked out how often we've been made to visit the old bitch? Since we were kids, sitting there, listening to her snide remarks, always being told to go and wash our hands . . . You hated it as much as I did.'

'If it meant hanging on to a fortune, I could put up with a damn sight more than that. You've no business wrecking my chances as well as your own.'

'You really believe she'll cut us out?'

'Certain of it,' Hugh said flatly. 'Unless you can prevent the new will being signed, we've lost everything. Try concentrating on that instead of swilling beer with your fellow students. No more money, not a single penny!'

He gripped the wheel. Ahead was the illuminated entrance to a tube station. He pulled up outside. 'This is far enough.'

Calum was bewildered. 'What?'

'You can make your own way back to college. After what you've done, I don't trust myself. All I can think about are ways of breaking your fucking neck, so get out. Now.'

A foot taller and two stone heavier, Calum didn't argue. He stood on the pavement hunched inside his coat collar, frowning because events had moved too quickly.

'What will you do?' he asked Hugh.

'About what?'

'About that three thou, of course. You need it badly, don't you?'

'Mind your own business.'

'I really will go and see her, Hugh. I've been an idiot but I'll go on my knees if I have to. Thursday – I have

Thursday off this week. She can't take it away now – we've been brought up to *expect* that money. I'll go round and I'll kiss her feet, anything.' He bent closer, imploring him, 'Will you go and see her, as well? Tell her I didn't mean it. She can see through me but she trusts you. When you qualified as a doctor, she was very impressed.'

'I told you, she's not a fool; she knows you meant every single word.'

'Hugh, we can't afford to lose that money.'

'A pity you didn't think of that before.' Behind him, a taxi hooted. Calum clung to the car door.

'Please, Hugh. It won't work unless we both go and see her. You're right, we need to get there before she has time to change anything. Shall I phone that solicitor chap Stuart and explain—'

'For Christ's sake, NO! Haven't you got any sense at all?'

'Sorry, sorry.'

The taxi hooted again. Hugh released the clutch and Calum stepped back to let him go. Glancing in the rear-view mirror, Hugh found himself thinking how wonderful life would be without either Calum or Aunt Mildred to screw things up. However, it would take more than a miracle to bring that about.

It was his weekend on duty. From Friday night through to eight o'clock on Monday morning. Hurrying into the hospital out of the sleet, Hugh sent up a prayer that the 'take' would be low tonight. It wasn't likely, given the worsening weather. Always a harbinger of traffic pile-ups, these would be followed by urgent appeals from casualty for spare beds.

He made his way to ward B6. The human gut was his speciality, or rather it would be if ever he reached consultant status. Not that he stood a chance of that with the threat of bankruptcy hanging over him. It interfered with every thought process. Even as he stared at an illuminated X-ray, red figures would superimpose themselves: the amount of his overdraft coming between him and his patient.

How could he have been expected to know that interest rates and mortgages would rise so astronomically? Five years ago the bank was urging him to borrow money. He'd taken a loan – the student grant was ridiculously small. But when it came to repayments, his initial salary was so low, the debt outstripped it. So he took each of his credit cards to the limit, it seemed the only sensible thing to do.

The first warning letter made him pause and add everything up – Hugh couldn't believe the incredible total. He began to look for excuses, he kept telling himself if only he could clear the debt he was bound to become a better doctor. Mildred could easily spare three thousand pounds. Damn Calum, damn him to hell!

Tonight, the ward routine soothed him. He spent longer than he needed at the nursing station, checking patients' notes on the computer, ordering TPRs on one elderly woman who was losing the battle against an encroaching tumour.

It was quiet, there weren't many visitors. Hugh went across to the woman, noting the pallor and increased puffiness of her face. He listened to her with half an ear as he checked her charts.

Aunt Mildred was always full of complaints against her doctor; it was a pleasure to listen to Mrs Hamilton.

Not only was she grateful, she amused him.

He summoned the staff nurse to discuss a particular drug. 'Is she responding to the increased dose?' Staff shook her head. 'We'd better try something else, I don't like the look of her.' He returned to his patient. 'May I examine you, Mrs Hamilton?'

Seventy years old, she smiled coquettishly. 'Help yourself, young man.'

'It's your bowels we're concerned about.'

'Not again!' She pulled a face. 'What a nuisance I am to you all.'

'It's not your fault. The laxatives aren't working as well as we'd hoped.' His mind was playing tricks: he imagined it was Aunt Mildred lying there and only Mrs Hamilton's gasp brought him back to reality. 'Sorry! That's a bit tender?'

Mrs Hamilton released her breath. 'Uh-huh.'

'We need to start things moving again.'

'Senna pods,' she challenged. 'Nothing better. I should know. My grandmother dished them out regularly.'

Hugh smiled, his heart beating wildly as an idea began to take shape. 'I think we'll try something a little more modern.' At the nurses' station he spoke quietly, 'Picolax.'

'Poor soul! You are going to warn her?'

'Of course.' Hugh ducked under the curtains once more. 'This medicine is very strong, Mrs Hamilton. We'll give you a dose tomorrow. When you need to go to the bathroom, take a book. It's usually very effective.'

'Sounds formidable! How about *War and Peace*, will that be long enough?' Chuckling, Hugh entered up the dose on her chart – in pencil – and initialled it. Much to the staff nurse's surprise, he said, 'If I'm free, I'll come and give it to her myself.'

On Thursday, when Calum arrived at Aunt Mildred's for his promised visit, Frances the housekeeper was on the look-out. 'She's still terribly upset. We've had to have the doctor twice this week.'

'I don't suppose she was well enough to see Mr Stuart?'

'Yes, she was. Mildred said that business was too important to leave unfinished. You know what it was about?'

Calum sighed. 'I'm afraid so, yes.'

'*You* shouldn't've been so rude. It's Dr Hugh I feel sorry for.' She waited impatiently as he hung his coat and scarf on the hallstand. 'Well? Don't you want to hear what Mildred's GP said?'

'Yes, of course.'

'Mildred has to take things very, very easy. No visitors. I was in two minds whether I ought to let you come today.'

Calum switched on the charm. 'I'm not "visitors", I'm family. Don't worry, I shan't upset her again. Here, do you think she'll like these?' He waved the freesias under Frances's nose.

She sniffed. 'Funerals. That's what they remind me of. Still, it's the thought that counts.'

As they climbed the stairs, he asked casually, 'Has Hugh been?'

'No.' She was curious. 'You've both become very attentive all of a sudden.'

'We were worried. Aunt Mildred told us her pills had been changed. Hugh was worried her angina was worse.'

Frances's eyebrows shot up. 'If you were that worried, it's a pity you upset her so badly.' She tapped on the bedroom door. 'It's Mr Calum – can he come in?'

An hour later when he came downstairs, Calum was whistling. Frances hurried through from the kitchen to meet him. 'You haven't tired her?'

'Certainly not. I've persuaded her to cancel Stuart's visit tonight, though. Hugh phoned me at college and said he might come over. Signing the new will can wait.'

At the tube station, Calum dialled Hugh's number. 'Hi, it's me. I've been to see her.'

'Did you grovel?'

'Absolutely. Your turn now. I've managed to defer Stuart till next week. If you butter her up as well, it might do the trick—'

'Tonight isn't very convenient—'

'Hugh! You said you would see her tonight.'

'I said "might". How long were you there?'

'An hour, maybe longer.'

'Did you take her any flowers?'

'Of course. Flowers, chocolates – and I sent Frances to wait downstairs so Milly and I could have a proper heart to heart. She even let me kiss her goodbye. I bet by the end of the week she tears up the draft of that new will.'

At his end of the line, Hugh's heart thumped with excitement. 'Let's hope so. Okay Calum, you've done well. I'll go round and see her.'

'Great!'

Hugh was apologetic to Frances. 'I know Calum's been. I certainly don't want to tire her.'

'I was just about to take her supper up.'

'May I sit with her while she has it?'

Frances sniffed. 'If she's no objection.' Hugh followed her through to the kitchen, to collect the tray.

'I saw these cans on the WVS trolley. I remembered how Aunt Mildred used to enjoy them.'

Frances looked at the collection of soft drinks. 'Dandelion and burdock . . . sarsaparilla. Fancy you remembering. She's been complaining of feeling thirsty. Maybe it's her new pills.'

'Why don't we give her one to drink this evening?'

She handed him a crystal tumbler and Hugh admired the elegantly set tray.

'I try and make it look nice, to tempt her.'

'She'd be lost without you.'

Frances was embarrassed. 'We suit one another, always have . . . I'm sorry about the quarrel. Especially as it was Mr Calum who was rude and you've suffered by it. I tried to tell her but she wouldn't listen.'

'Let's not spoil this evening by talking about it.'

Frances picked up the tray. 'She's never treated you fairly, since you were both little. I told Mr Stuart when he came – always Calum this, Calum that because he had the charm. And now you stand to lose everything because of what Calum said to her.'

Hugh hid any hurt behind the casual question, 'When is Stuart due to call again?'

'She's put him off till next week. You won't stay too long tonight, will you? She'll need a good night's sleep if she's to be clear-headed in the morning.'

Inside the invalid's room, Hugh kissed his aunt's cheek and retreated to the window seat. He made soothing conversation as the food disappeared, and tried not to watch as Mildred drained the tumbler.

'Lovely, Hugh. Just what I needed.'

He said awkwardly, 'I'm so glad. I'll leave you now. You shouldn't overdo things. Two visitors is quite enough for one day.' Mildred nodded drowsily.

'Calum has apologised.'

'So I should hope—'

'I didn't believe a word of it. Good-night, Hugh. Thank you for the drink.'

Downstairs, he said to Frances, 'Those flowers by her bed – I think you should remove them. The pollen, it could irritate her breathing.'

Frances was immediately anxious. 'I'll do it straight away. How do you think she is? She was ever so tired after Mr Calum left.'

Hugh shook his head solemnly. 'Next time, I'd interrupt them if I were you. Ten minutes is enough.'

'I'll remember. She's having difficulty walking just now as well.'

'That sounds like poor circulation – would you like me to have a word with her GP?'

'If you would. I'd hate to think . . . We've been together a long time.'

He patted her hand. 'No need to be gloomy, Frances. Aunt Mildred is a tough old bird even if she has got a weak heart. Don't forget those flowers.'

In the early hours of the following morning, the GP surveyed his former patient, lying on the floor of her bedroom amid a vast amount of her own excreta. 'What a terrible thing to happen!'

Frances's tears overflowed. 'She was always so particular about being clean. It's dreadful to think of her lying there, not able to get to the lav. . .'

'A most fastidious lady.'

'She couldn't reach her pills, she must've fallen getting out of bed, trying to reach them.'

'Maybe . . . ' The medical man was thoughtful.

'Do you think it was the pollen made her giddy? Dr Hugh said I was to move the flowers.'

'Oh?' Downstairs, the GP surveyed the freesias. 'It's an enormous bunch. Who gave her these?'

'Calum. He's the one at agricultural college. He came round to say how sorry he was. You remember Mildred told you about the row, and the fact she was changing her will?' The GP nodded. 'I reckon Calum hoped his aunt would leave things just as they were.'

'Of course.'

'Dr Hugh was worried the pollen could affect her breathing.'

'Tell me what he said.'

The details of the two visits emerged. At the finish the GP declared he wasn't happy to issue a death certificate until the freesias had been examined. Frances must repeat her tale to the police. Certainly he had never had a patient whose bowels had erupted with such volcanic force – no wonder Mildred's heart had finally given way, under the strain.

There was a range of toxic substances at the agricultural college. Traces of some of them were on Calum's overalls. The freesias were declared innocent but Frances kept assuring the police that Calum had spent an hour alone with his aunt and had been urging her to sniff the flowers as soon as he arrived.

When the case came to court, the forensic expert appearing for the Crown pointed out that only a small amount of one of the toxic powders, mixed in with pollen, could be fatal if inhaled. Under cross-examination, he had to admit that so far nothing toxic had been found despite microscopic examination of the tissues, but the jury weren't particularly interested. They were much more smitten with the idea of pollen being used to conceal other nefarious substances.

Evidence of Calum's indebtedness was plentiful, as was his confident assumption he would inherit a large sum on his aunt's demise. Finally, Mr Stuart the solicitor provided the perfect motive by describing his client's account of the quarrel, instigated by the accused, resulting in the new – alas unsigned – will. When the latter was summarised and read aloud, several of the jury nodded their heads. The men were particularly glad that anyone as good-looking as that should receive his come-uppance.

Calum's defence was that Hugh had a far greater need of money than he did. Women on the jury didn't like him accusing his brother. When Hugh appeared to answer the charges, his very ordinariness, his obvious concern for his aunt, made a very good impression.

He had taken care, with the help of an astute bank manager who fully understood his client's expectations, to spread the three thousand pound debt over a very long period of time so that the monthly payments were almost insignificant. Police and jury thought so, anyway. Finally, when Frances contrasted the behaviour of the two brothers during that fateful visit, Hugh was practically home and dry.

He had to listen as Calum hurled accusations at him from the box. Eventually, the judge gestured for the prisoner to be removed from the dock while the final details of the case were wrapped up.

The police reported briskly that drugs were scrupulously administered at the hospital, all but one of Hugh's prescriptions could be accounted for, and none of them had spotted that particular lapse because the staff nurse hadn't drawn their attention to it.

Later, the staff nurse spoke to Hugh.

'I noticed you wrote Mrs Hamilton up for Lactulose as well as Picolax last time I was on nights – you didn't give her both, did you?'

'Good heavens, no! I changed my mind. I decided Picolax was too strong but I'd opened the packet by then. After giving her the Lactulose, I flushed the contents of the Picolax packet down the loo. You'd gone off duty – I'm sorry I forgot to mention it.'

'That's okay. I assumed you'd made the change. It was entered as Lactulose, not Picolax on her chart – at least you remembered to alter that.'

Hugh thanked her profusely for pointing out the mistake – and hoped to God she wouldn't blab about the chart to anyone else. He lowered his voice. 'Mrs Hamilton is a very brave lady. We'll use suppositories from now on when she needs a bit of help.' Staff responded with an understanding smile; a caring person, Dr Wilson, one of the best. Everyone felt really sorry for him when his brother was sentenced to life imprisonment.

After he'd gone, the probationer asked, 'What's Picolax?'

'It's a fiendish laxative. If you have a full dose, you've just about time to get to the loo and there you stay until you're cleaned out. You've no control over your bowels

– it's terrible, absolute dynamite.'

'Wow!' The probationer giggled. 'What does it taste like? Gunpowder?'

'No, that's the joke; it's just like sarsaparilla.'

Facing the Music

An Inspector Rebus Story

Ian Rankin

Facing the Music

An Inspector Rebus Story

An unmarked police car.

Interesting phrase that. Inspector John Rebus's car, punch-drunk and weather-beaten, scarred and mauled, would still merit description as 'unmarked', despite the copious evidence to the contrary. Oily-handed mechanics stifled grins whenever he waddled into a forecourt. Garage proprietors adjusted the thick gold rings on their fingers and reached for the calculator.

Still, there were times when the old war-horse came in handy. It might or might not be 'unmarked'; unremarkable it certainly was. Even the most cynical law-breaker would hardly expect CID to spend their time sitting around in a breaker's-yard special. Rebus's car was a must for undercover work, the only problem coming if the villains decided to make a run for it. Then, even the most elderly and infirm could outpace it.

'But it's a stayer,' Rebus would say in mitigation.

He sat now, the driving-seat so used to his shape that it formed a mould around him, stroking the steering-wheel with his hands. There was a loud sigh from the passenger seat, and Detective Sergeant Brian Holmes repeated his question.

'Why have we stopped?'

Rebus looked around him. They were parked by the side of Queensferry Street, only a couple of hundred yards from Princes Street's west end. It was early afternoon, overcast but dry. The gusts of wind blowing in from the Firth of Forth were probably keeping the rain away. The corner of Princes Street, where Fraser's department store and the Caledonian Hotel tried to outstare one another, caught the winds and whipped them against unsuspecting shoppers, who could be seen, dazed and numb, making their way afterwards along Queensferry Street, in search of coffee and shortcake. Rebus gave the pedestrians a look of pity. Holmes sighed again. He could murder a pot of tea and some fruit scones with butter.

'Do you know, Brian,' Rebus began, 'in all the years I've been in Edinburgh, I've never been called to any sort of a crime on this street.' He slapped the steering-wheel for emphasis. 'Not once.'

'Maybe they should put up a plaque,' suggested Holmes.

Rebus almost smiled. 'Maybe they should.'

'Is that why we're sitting here? You want to break your duck?' Holmes glanced into a tea-shop window, then away again quickly, licking dry lips. 'It might take a while, you know,' he said.

'It might, Brian. But then again . . .'

Rebus tapped out a tattoo on the steering-wheel. Holmes was beginning to regret his own enthusiasm. Hadn't Rebus tried to deter him coming out for this drive? Not that they'd driven much. But anything, Holmes reasoned, was better than catching up on paperwork. Well, just about anything.

'What's the longest time you've been on a stake-out?' he asked, making conversation.

'A week,' said Rebus. 'Protection racket run from a pub down near Powderhall. It was a joint operation with Trading Standards. We spent five days pretending to be on the broo, playing pool all day.'

'Did you get a result?'

'We beat them at pool,' Rebus said.

There was a yell from a shop doorway, just as a young man was sprinting across the road in front of their car. The young man was carrying a black metal box. The person who'd called out did so again.

'Stop him! Thief! Stop him!'

The man in the shop doorway was waving, pointing towards the sprinter. Holmes looked towards Rebus, seemed about to say something, but decided against it. 'Come on then!' he said.

Rebus started the car's engine, signalled, and moved out into the traffic. Holmes was focusing through the windscreen. 'I can see him. Put your foot down!'

' "Put your foot down, *sir*," ' Rebus said calmly. 'Don't worry, Brian.'

'Hell, he's turning into Randolph Place.'

Rebus signalled again, brought the car across the

oncoming traffic, and turned into the dead end that was Randolph Place. Only, while it was a dead end for cars, there were pedestrian passages either side of West Register House. The young man, carrying the narrow box under his arm, turned into one of the passages. Rebus pulled to a halt. Holmes had the car door open before it had stopped, and leapt out, ready to follow on foot.

'Cut him off!' he yelled, meaning for Rebus to drive back on to Queensferry Street, around Hope Street and into Charlotte Square, where the passage emerged.

' "Cut him off, *sir*," ' mouthed Rebus.

He did a careful three-point turn, and just as carefully moved back out into traffic held to a crawl by traffic lights. By the time he reached Charlotte Square and the front of West Register House, Holmes was shrugging his shoulders and flapping his arms. Rebus pulled to a stop beside him.

'Did you see him?' Holmes asked, getting into the car.

'No.'

'Where have you been anyway?'

'A red light.'

Holmes looked at him as though he were mad. Since when had Inspector John Rebus stopped for a red light? 'Well, I've lost him anyway.'

'Not your fault, Brian.'

Holmes looked at him again. 'Right,' he agreed. 'So, back to the shop? What was it anyway?'

'Hi-fi shop, I think.'

Holmes nodded as Rebus moved off again into the traffic. Yes, the box had the look of a piece of hi-fi, some slim rack component. They'd find out at the shop. But instead of doing a circuit of Charlotte Square to take them back into Queensferry Street, Rebus signalled along George Street. Holmes, still catching his breath, looked around disbelieving.

'Where are we going?'

'I thought you were fed up with Queensferry Street. We're going back to the station.'

'*What*?'

'Back to the station.'

'But what about—?'

'Relax, Brian. You've got to learn not to fret so much.'

Holmes examined his superior's face. 'You're up to something,' he said at last.

Rebus turned and smiled. 'Took you long enough,' he said.

But whatever it was, Rebus wasn't telling. Back at the station, he went straight to the main desk.

'Any robberies, Alec?'

The desk officer had a few. The most recent was a snatch at a specialist hi-fi shop.

'We'll take that,' said Rebus. The desk officer blinked.

'It's not much, sir. Just a single item, thief did a runner.'

'Nevertheless, Alec,' said Rebus. 'A crime has been committed, and it's our duty to investigate it.' He turned to head back out to the car.

'Is he all right?' Alec asked Holmes.

Holmes was beginning to wonder, but decided to go along for the ride anyway.

'A cassette deck,' the proprietor explained. 'Nice model, too. Not top of the range, but nice. Top of the range stuff isn't kept out on the shop floor. We keep it in the demonstration rooms.'

Holmes was looking at the shelf where the cassette deck had rested. There were other decks either side of the gap, more expensive decks at that.

'Why would he choose that one?' Holmes asked.

'Eh?'

'Well, it's not the dearest, is it? And it's not even the closest to the door.'

The dealer shrugged. 'Kids these days, who can tell?' His thick hair was still tousled from where he had stood in the Queensferry Street wind-tunnel, yelling against the elements as passers-by stared at him.

'I take it you've got insurance, Mr Wardle?' The question came from Rebus, who was standing in front of a row of loudspeakers.

'Christ yes, and it costs enough.' Wardle shrugged. 'Look, it's okay. I know how it works. Points system, right? Anything under a four-point crime, and you lads don't bother. You just fill out the forms so I can claim from the insurance. What does this rate? One point? Two at the most?'

Rebus blinked, perhaps stunned by the use of the word 'lads' in connection with him.

'You've got the serial number, Mr Wardle,' he said at last. 'That'll give us a start. Then a description of the thief – that's more than we usually get in cases of shop-snatching. Meantime, you might move your stock a bit further back from the door and think about a common chain or circuit alarm so they can't be taken off their shelves. Okay?'

Wardle nodded.

'And be thankful,' mused Rebus. 'After all, it could've been worse. It could have been a ram-raider.' He picked up a CD case from where it sat on top of a machine: Mantovani and his Orchestra. 'Or even a critic,' said Rebus.

Back at the station, Holmes sat fuming like a readying volcano. Or at least like a tin of something flammable left for too long in the sun.

Whatever Rebus was up to, as per usual he wasn't saying. It infuriated Holmes. Now Rebus was off at a meeting in the Chief Super's office: nothing very important, just routine . . . like the snatch at the hi-fi shop.

Holmes played the scene through in his mind. The stationary car, causing an obstruction to the already slow movement of traffic. Then Wardle's cry, and the youth running across the road, jinking between cars. The youth had half-turned, giving Holmes a moment's view of a cheek speckled with acne, cropped spiky hair. A skinny runt of a sixteen-year-old in faded jeans and trainers. Pale blue windcheater with a lumberjack shirt hanging loose below its hemline.

And carrying a hi-fi component that was neither the easiest piece in the shop to steal, nor the dearest. Wardle had seemed relaxed about the whole affair. The insurance would cover it. An insurance scam: was that it? Was Rebus working on some insurance diddle on the q.t., maybe as a favour to some investigator from the Pru? Holmes hated the way his superior worked, like a greedy if talented footballer hogging the ball, dribbling past man after man, getting himself trapped beside the by-line but still refusing to pass the ball. Holmes had known a boy at school like that. One day, fed up, Holmes had scythed the smart-arse down, even though they'd been on the same side . . .

Rebus had known the theft would take place. Therefore, he'd been tipped off. Therefore, the thief had been set up. There was just one big *but* to the whole theory – Rebus had let the thief get away. It didn't make sense. It didn't make any sense at all.

'Right,' Holmes said, nodding to himself. 'Right you are, sir.' And with that, he went off to find the young offender files.

That evening, just after six, Rebus thought that since he was in the area anyway, he'd drop into Mr Wardle's home and report the lack of progress on the case. It might be that, time having passed, Wardle would remember something else about the snatch, some crucial detail. The description he'd been able to give of the thief had been next to useless. It was almost as though he didn't want the hassle, didn't want the thief caught. Well, maybe Rebus could jog his memory.

The radio came to life. It was a message from the station, a message from DS Holmes. And when Rebus heard it, he snarled and turned the car back around towards the city centre.

It was lucky for Holmes, so Rebus said, that the traffic had been heavy, the fifteen-minute journey back into town being time enough for him to calm down. They were in the CID room. Holmes was seated at his desk, hands clasped behind his head. Rebus was standing over him, breathing hard. On the desk sat a matt-black cassette deck.

'Serial numbers match,' Holmes said, 'just in case you were wondering.'

Rebus couldn't quite sound disinterested. 'How did you find him?'

With his hands still behind his head, Holmes managed a shrug. 'He was on file, sir. I just sat there flipping through them till I spotted him. That acne of his is as good as a tattoo. James Iain Bankhead, known to his friends as Jib. According to the file, you've arrested him a couple of times yourself in the past.'

'Jib Bankhead?' said Rebus, as though trying to place the name. 'Yes, rings a bell.'

'I'd have thought it'd ring a whole fire station, sir. You last arrested him three months ago.' Holmes made a show of consulting the file on his desk. 'Funny, you not recognising him . . . ' Holmes kept his eyes on the file.

'I must be getting old,' Rebus said.

Holmes looked up. 'So what now, sir?'

'Where is he?'

'Interview Room B.'

'Let him stay there then. Can't do any harm. Has he said anything?'

'Not a word. Mind you, he *did* seem surprised when I paid him a visit.'

'But he kept his mouth shut?'

Holmes nodded. 'So what now?' he repeated.

'Now,' said Rebus, 'you come along with me, Brian. I'll tell you all about it on the way . . .'

Wardle lived in a flat carved from a detached turn-of-the-century house on the south-east outskirts of the city. Rebus pressed the bell on the wall to the side of the substantial main door. After a moment, there was the muffled sound of footsteps, three clicks as locks were undone, and the door opened from within.

'Good evening, Mr Wardle,' said Rebus. 'I see you're

security-conscious at home at least.' Rebus was nodding towards the door, with its three separate keyholes, spy-hole and security chain.

'You can't be too—' Wardle broke off as he saw what Brian Holmes was carrying. 'The deck!'

'Good as new,' said Rebus, 'apart from a few fingerprints.'

Wardle opened the door wide. 'Come in, come in.'

They entered a narrow entrance hall which led to a flight of stairs. Obviously the ground floor of the house did not belong to Wardle. He was dressed much as he had been in the shop: denims too young for his years, an open-necked shirt louder than a Wee Free sermon, and brown moccasins.

'I can't believe it,' he said, leading them towards the stairs. 'I really can't. But you could have brought it round to the shop . . .'

'Well, sir, we were going to be passing anyway.' Rebus closed the door, noting the steel plate on its inner face. The door-surround too was reinforced with metal plates. Wardle turned and noticed Rebus's interest.

'Wait till you see the hi-fi, Inspector. It'll all become clear.'

They could already hear the music. The bass was vibrating each step of the stairs.

'You must have sympathetic neighbours,' Rebus remarked.

'She's ninety-two,' said Wardle. 'Deaf as a post. I went round to explain to her about the hi-fi just after I moved in. She couldn't hear a word I was saying.'

They were at the top of the stairs now, where a smaller hallway led into a huge open-plan living-room and kitchen. A sofa and two chairs had been pushed hard back against one wall, and there was nothing but space between them and the opposite wall, where the hi-fi system sat, with large floor-standing speakers either side of it. One rack comprised half a dozen black boxes, boasting nothing to Rebus's eye but a single red light.

'Amplifiers,' Wardle explained, turning down the music.

'What, all of them?'

'Pre-amp and power supply, plus an amp for each driver.'

Holmes had rested the cassette-deck on the floor, but Wardle moved it away immediately.

'Spoils the sound,' he said, 'if there's an extra piece of gear in the room.'

Holmes and Rebus stared at one another. Wardle was in his element now. 'Want to hear something? What's your taste?'

'Rolling Stones?' Rebus asked.

'*Sticky Fingers, Exile, Let it Bleed*?'

'That last one,' said Rebus.

Wardle went over to where a twenty-foot row of LPs was standing against the wall beneath the window.

'I thought those went out with the Ark,' said Holmes.

Wardle smiled. 'You mean with the CD. No, vinyl's still the best. Sit down.' He went over to the turntable and took off the LP he'd been playing. Rebus and Holmes sat. Holmes looked to Rebus, who nodded. Holmes got up again.

'Actually, could I use your loo?' he asked.

'First right out on the landing,' said Wardle. Holmes left the room. 'Any particular track, Inspector?'

' "Gimme Shelter",' stated Rebus. Wardle nodded

agreement, set the needle on the disc, rose to his feet, and turned up the volume. 'Something to drink?' he asked. The room exploded into a wall of sound. Rebus had heard the phrase 'wall of sound' before. Well, here he was with his nose pressed against it.

'A whisky, please,' he yelled. Wardle tipped his head towards the hall. 'Same for him.' Wardle nodded and went off towards the kitchen area. Pinned to the sofa as he was, Rebus looked around the room. He had eyes for everything but the hi-fi. Not that there was much to see. A small coffee-table whose surface seemed to be covered with arcana to do with the hi-fi system, cleaning-brushes and such like. There were some nice-looking prints on the wall. Actually, one looked like a real painting rather than a print: the surface of a swimming-pool, someone moving through the depths. But no TV, no shelves, no books, no knick-knacks, no family photos. Rebus knew Wardle was divorced. He also knew Wardle drove a Y-registered Porsche 911. He knew quite a lot about Wardle, but not yet enough . . .

A healthy glass of whisky was handed to him. Wardle placed another on the floor for Holmes, then returned to the kitchen and came back with a glass for himself. He sat down next to Rebus.

'What do you think?'

'Fantastic,' Rebus called back.

Wardle grinned.

'How much would this lot cost me?' Rebus asked, hoping Wardle wouldn't notice how long Holmes had been out of the room.

'About twenty-five K.'

'You're joking. My flat didn't cost that.'

Wardle just laughed. But he was glancing towards

the living-room door. He looked as though he might be about to say something, when the door opened and Holmes came in, rubbing his hands as though drying them off. He smiled, sat, and toasted Wardle with his glass. Wardle went over to the amplifier to turn down the volume. Holmes nodded towards Rebus. Rebus toasted no one in particular and finished his drink. The volume dipped.

'What was that?' Holmes asked.

'*Let it Bleed*.'

'I thought my ears would.'

Wardle laughed. He seemed to be in a particularly good mood. Maybe it was because of the cassette-deck.

'Listen,' he said, 'how the hell did you get that deck back so quickly?'

Holmes was about to say something, but Rebus beat him to it. 'It was abandoned.'

'Abandoned?'

'At the bottom of a flight of stairs on Queen Street,' Rebus went on. He had risen to his feet. Holmes took the hint and, eyes twisted shut, gulped down his whisky. 'So you see, sir, we were just lucky, that's all. Just lucky.'

'Well, thanks again,' said Wardle. 'If you ever want some hi-fi, drop into the shop. I'm sure a discount might be arranged.'

'We'll bear that in mind, sir,' said Rebus. 'Just don't expect me to put my flat on the market . . .'

Back at the station, Rebus first of all had Jib released, then went to his office, where he spread the files out across his desk, while Holmes pulled over a chair. Then they both sat, reading aloud from lists. The lists were of stolen goods, high quality stuff stolen in the dead of night by real professionals. The hauls – highly selective hauls – came from five addresses, the homes of well-paid middle-class people, people with things well worth the stealing.

Five robberies, all at dead of night, alarm systems disconnected. Art objects had been taken, antiques, in one case an entire collection of rare European stamps. The house-breakings had occurred at more or less monthly intervals, and all within a twenty-mile radius of central Edinburgh. The connection between them? Rebus had explained it to Holmes on their way to Wardle's flat.

'Nobody could see *any* connection, apart from the fact that the five victims worked in the west end. The Chief Super asked me to take a look. Guess what I found? They'd all had smart new hi-fi systems installed. Up to six months before the break-ins. Systems bought from Queensferry Audio and installed by Mr Wardle.'

'So he'd know what was in each house?' Holmes had said.

'And he'd be able to give the alarm system a look-over while he was there, too.'

'Could just be coincidence.'

'I know.'

Oh yes, Rebus knew. He knew he had only the hunch, the coincidence. He had no proof, no evidence of any kind. Certainly nothing that would gain him a search warrant, as the Chief Super had been good enough to confirm, knowing damned well that Rebus would take it further anyway. Not that this concerned the Chief Super, so long as Rebus worked alone, and didn't tell his superiors what he was up to. That way, it was Rebus's neck in the noose, Rebus's pension on the line.

Rebus guessed his only hope was that Wardle had kept some of the stolen pieces, that some of the stuff was still on his premises. He'd already had a young DC go into Queensferry Audio posing as a would-be buyer. The DC had gone in four times in all, once to buy some tapes, then to look at hi-fi, then to spend an hour in one of the demo rooms, and finally just for a friendly chat . . . He'd reported back to Rebus that the place was clean. No signs of any stolen merchandise, no locked rooms or cupboards . . .

So then Rebus had persuaded a uniformed constable to pose as a Neighbourhood Watch supervisor. He had visited Wardle at home, not getting past the downstairs hallway. But he'd been able to report that the place was 'like Fort Knox, metal door and all'. Rebus had had experience of steel-reinforced doors: they were favoured by drug dealers, so that when police came calling with a sledgehammer for invitation, the dealers would have time enough to flush everything away.

But a hi-fi dealer with a steel door . . . Well, that was a new one. True, twenty-five grand's worth of hi-fi was an investment worth protecting. But there were limits. Not that Rebus suspected Wardle of actually doing the breaking and entering himself. No, he just passed the information on to the men Rebus really wanted, the gang. But Wardle was the only means of getting at them . . .

Finally, in desperation, Rebus had turned to Jib. And Jib had done what he was told, meaning Rebus now owed him a large favour. It was all highly irregular; unlawful, if it came to it. If anyone found out . . . well, Rebus would be making the acquaintance of his local broo office. Which was why, as he explained to Holmes, he'd been keeping so quiet about it.

The plan was simple. Jib would run off with something, anything, watched by Rebus to make sure nothing went wrong – such as a daring citizen's arrest by one or more passers-by. Later, Rebus would turn up at the shop to investigate the theft. Then later still, he would arrive at Wardle's flat, ostensibly to report the lack of progress. If a further visit was needed, the cassette-deck would be found. But now he had Holmes's help, so one visit only should suffice, one man keeping Wardle busy while the other sniffed around the rooms in the flat.

They sat now, poring over the lists, trying to match what Holmes had seen in Wardle's two bedrooms with what had been reported stolen from the five luxury homes.

'Carriage clock,' read Rebus, 'nineteenth-century Japanese cigar box, seventeenth-century prints of Edinburgh by James Gordon, a Swarbreck lithograph . . .'

Holmes shook his head at the mention of each, then read from one of his own lists. 'Ladies and gents' Longines watches, a Hockney print, Cartier pen, first-edition set of the Waverley novels, Ming vase, Dresden pieces . . . ' He looked up. 'Would you believe, there's even a case of champagne.' He looked down again and read: ' "Louis Roederer Cristal 1985". Value put at £500. That's forty quid a bottle.'

'Bet you're glad you're a lager man,' said Rebus. He sighed. 'Does none of this mean anything to you, Brian?'

Holmes shook his head. 'Nothing like any of this in either of the bedrooms.'

Rebus cursed under his breath. 'Hold on,' he said. 'What about that print?'

'Which one? The Hockney?'

'Yes, have we got a photo of it?'

'Just this,' said Holmes, extracting from the file a page torn from an art gallery's catalogue. He handed it to Rebus, who studied the picture. 'Why?'

'Why?' echoed Rebus. 'Because you sat with this painting in front of your nose on Wardle's living-room wall. I thought it was a real painting, but this is it all right.' He tapped the sheet of paper. 'It says here the print's limited to fifty impressions. What number is the stolen one?'

Holmes looked down the list. 'Forty-four.'

'Right,' said Rebus. 'That should be easy enough to confirm.' He checked his watch. 'What time are you expected home?'

Holmes was shaking his head. 'Never mind that. If you're going back to Wardle's flat, I'm coming too.'

'Come on then.'

It was only as they were leaving the office that Holmes thought to ask: 'What if it isn't the same number on the print?'

'Then we'll just have to face the music,' said Rebus.

But as it turned out, the only one facing the music was Wardle, and he sang beautifully. A pity, Rebus mused later, that he hadn't arranged for a discount on a new hi-fi system first. He'd just have to wait for Queensferry Audio's closing down sale . . .

In the Bluebell Wood

Julian Symons

In the Bluebell Wood

Lance could not remember a time before he knew about King Arthur, the Knights of the Round Table, and the fact that he had been named for the most famous of them. The bluebell wood too had its place in this. It was his father who told him the stories, about the coming of Arthur, the beauty of Guinevere and her love of Lancelot. At first the stories were from a big book called the *Morte D'Arthur*, but then they came from poems, poems called the *Idylls of the King* written by a man named Tennyson, which was his father's surname and, as he learned, his own.

In adolescence, thinking back, he remembered being in bed, fingers twitching the sheets, his father's face above him uttering passionately words he did not quite understand – *honour, chivalry* – and phrases that stayed in his mind even though he did not understand their meaning – 'live pure, speak true, right wrong, follow the

King – else, wherefore born?' There was nothing in the poems about a bluebell wood, yet when he closed his eyes after the readings he quite distinctly saw himself, Lancelot, riding with Guinevere, dismounting at a stile, then walking hand in hand with her down a grassy path to the dimness of a wood carpeted with bluebells . . . And when he opened his eyes the words flowed round him still:

> Many a bard, without offence,
> Has linked our names together in his lay,
> Lancelot, the flower of bravery, Guinevere
> The pearl of beauty

The face of the story-teller loomed large above him, eyes magnified by round spectacles. He knew the rough feel of army cloth on his bare arm, the smell of tobacco. His father was home on leave during the War. What was the War, why did his father wear a uniform and not armour, what did he do when he left home again, did he follow the King?

Nothing like that, his mother said. Anyway, she added laughing, if Lionel did follow the King he'd soon lose sight of him. 'Your father's blind as a bat without his glasses. He does hush-hush work.'

'What's hush-hush?'

'Secret. Work that keeps him away. Very important.'

'For the King?'

'I suppose you could say that. For King and country.'

They lived on the fringe of London, in an area that had missed almost all the wartime bombing. They had a little red brick house with a tiny front garden and one at the back that was slightly bigger. The house next door was just the same, and the one next door to that, and so on down the road. 'Only way to tell 'em apart is by numbers,' his mother Esme said. 'Know what we are?' she asked neighbours. 'Rabbits in hutches, that's what.'

'Good job we don't breed like 'em.'

'You can take precautions.'

They went off into fits of laughter. Esme was small, dark, quick moving. The neighbour, whose husband was fighting somewhere in Italy, was named Louise. They saw a lot of each other. When Lance came home from the school that was just three minutes' walk away, Louise would often be in the kitchen. Esme got his tea and they sat with him while he ate it, both smoking so that the room became blue with it, and talking incomprehensibly. He imagined Lancelot riding through those blue mists, freeing a fair maiden, then meeting Guinevere, they crossed the stile . . . Fragments of phrases came through to him.

' . . . Dead and alive hole . . . see more life in a factory . . . you got a kid you got a millstone round your neck . . .'

His father came home on weekend leave from the hush-hush job quite often, and read from the *Idylls* about Gareth and Lynette, Merlin and Vivien, and what he loved most, Lancelot and Guinevere. Lying in bed, waiting for his father to come upstairs, he heard voices raised, his mother's sometimes almost a shriek.

It was when his father was at the hush-hush job that the visitor came. He was there when Lance came back from school, a tall smiling man who wore a much smarter uniform than his father's, and one with stars which the boy knew meant he was an officer, while his father had only the stripes of a sergeant. The officer's name was Pierre, and Esme said he belonged to the Free French. Pierre made pennies and a shilling come out of his ears, and gave them to Lance. Then Esme said she'd arranged for him to have tea and play with Tim Collins, who lived a few doors down the road. The arrangement was unusual, almost unknown.

'I don't want to.' He began to cry.

Esme's temper was short. 'You'll do as you're told. You're going out to tea, is that a reason to be a cry baby?'

'Look here.' Pierre produced another shilling from his ear. 'Why don't you and your friend Tim see what you can buy with this?'

When he was home again his mother said: 'I was ashamed of you, crying just because you'd been asked out to tea.' He made no reply. 'Did you like Pierre?'

'Don't know.'

'He's just a friend. Of Louise's really. No need to mention him to your father. Did you hear me?' He nodded. 'Say yes when you're spoken to.'

'Yes.'

He said nothing to his father, even though he saw Pierre again more than once – just leaving as he came home from school, in the kitchen where he made jokes when they had tea together, once coming out of the bathroom wearing only shirt and pants. Did Lance understand what was happening? That was a question he never asked himself later on. At the time he was simply puzzled when Tim Collins, who never had been a friend of his, said his mother was having it off with a frog. Having what off? he wondered, and he had only seen pictures of frogs.

But although he said nothing he did compare the round-shouldered goggle-eyed figure in a uniform that never seemed to fit properly with upright trim smiling Pierre, whose trousers had a crease of knife-edge sharpness, and who could make shillings come out of his ears. Then suddenly the War was over, there was a big party in their road with dancing and drinking and lots of food, including things he had never seen like bananas, all set out on trestle tables. Pierre was seen no more, someone said he had gone back to France, and good riddance. Esme went around red eyed, and shorter tempered than usual. And Lionel Tennyson, no longer Sergeant Tennyson, was demobbed, came home, went back to his work in the Ministry. Yes, he said to Lance who was now in primary school, the War was really over.

'And we won. We beat the bad men like Sir Mordred, the good knights won.' By this time Lance was reading the *Idylls* himself, knew some of the exciting bits by heart.

' "The good knights won",' his father echoed. They were in the bow-windowed living-room. On the walls were reproductions of Victorian pictures, one showing the passing of Arthur, another Lancelot and Guinevere. He stood, in full armour, looking at his drawn sword, she knelt and gazed at him yearningly, her long fair hair around her face and falling to her waist, feet showing below the pure white of her robe. A silver-plated figure of King Arthur stood on the mahogany sideboard, drawing the magic sword Excalibur from its scabbard.

Yes, his father said, but it was not like King Arthur. 'Bombs instead of swords nowadays. More's the pity.'

'But the stories are all really true, aren't they?'

'Oh yes, yes, yes.' His father became excited, as he had been when reading aloud about Lancelot's deeds as an unknown knight at a tournament. 'They are all true, and you must never forget them. That's why you were named Lancelot.' He still read to his son sometimes at night, until Esme said the boy was too old for that now, it just encouraged him to be childish.

Afterwards Lance remembered these years of adolescence as an idyll in his own life. His father went each day to the Ministry and he went to school, got good reports, came back, did his homework and then read a romantic story like *Kidnapped* or *Under The Red Robe*. Later, in bed, he read the *Idylls*. Afterwards he tried to remember something Esme had said that showed dissatisfaction with this life, which for her was one of keeping house and cooking, but could recall nothing. There were none of the arguments he had heard downstairs when he was a child, she was meticulous as ever in seeing that meals were cooked on time, and in cleaning the house so that everything smelt of furniture polish.

Then one day she was gone. He came home to find tea on the table, bread and margarine, jam, scones she had made the previous day. He ate, washed up the things, settled down in the kitchen to his homework. When his father came home he said: 'Mum's out'. Mr Tennyson nodded, went upstairs, came down again five minutes later looking paler than usual, eyes behind thick glasses vacant as those of a fish. He sat down at the kitchen table, put his head in his hands, said to his son: 'She's taken all her things, everything. Gone.'

Lance was aware of his open mouth, closed it, said gone where? His father shook his head. 'When will she be coming back?'

'She isn't. You remember a man coming round two or

three weeks ago selling vacuum cleaners, or trying to?' Lance nodded. 'She's gone off with him. With a vacuum cleaner salesman.'

Lance put an arm round his father's shoulder. 'We can manage. Until she comes back.'

'She hates me, she says so in the letter. She'll never come back.' He raised a face wet with tears.

Esme didn't come back. And Mr Tennyson was quite incapable of managing. He burned meat and under-cooked vegetables, and since these were days before frozen foods they ate mostly out of tins. A woman who came in to do housework stole the few valuable things in the house, including the figure of King Arthur. Within a year the house had been sold and they moved into a small flat in the same area, but in a main road with lorries rattling by day and night. It was cheaper, less trouble, a cleaner came in a couple of hours each week, there was nothing much to steal. The Victorian prints of Arthur, Lancelot and Guinevere remained, although they looked out of place in the tiny living-room. There was no garden, and Mr Tennyson loved gardening. One day Lance asked what the secret work was that his father had done in the War.

'Helping to decode German messages. I'm a statistician, you see, good at analysing sets of numbers and figures. I was one of a team. What we did was really quite important.'

He sensed that this was delicate ground. 'But no fighting?'

'No fighting. I wouldn't have been much good at it. Like you, I can't see very well.' And Lance, looking in the mirror, saw that his glasses were almost as thick as his father's, his face the same moon shape. So what was his father's job now at the Ministry, was it still important work?

'Not really. Mostly paperwork. Ordering materials for use in government contracts, then following them through, checking prices, keeping suppliers on their toes about delivery, making sure they don't overcharge. It's secure, you see, that's the great thing. When you're in the civil service you have a job for life. I'm not a do-er, you know, but I love the stories, and I wanted you to love them too. And of course there's my name, that made me read the poems first of all. I was called Lionel, and Lionel Tennyson was a great cricketer, captain of England. But I'm a reader, not a do-er. It was a kind of separate life for me.'

A separate life, a secret life. Perhaps that conversation was the beginning for Lance of the secret life in which he was somebody different from the awkward teenager who looked uneasily at the world through round spectacles, was shy with girls and no good at games. In the secret life Judy, who burst into laughter when he asked if she would like to go with him to a pop concert, said wistfully that she thought Lancelot was a beautiful name, and wished she was called Guinevere and not dull Judy. 'To me you will always be Guinevere,' he said as she leaned towards him, opening her lips for the kiss.

The closest of Lance's few friends at school was Rod Williams, who told all sorts of tales about his father's adventures as a scrap dealer. 'What's your father do?' Rod asked. 'Office job, isn't it, pen pushing?'

'Not really. It's hush-hush work.'

'But what's he *do*?'

'He's an agent.'

'What, MI5?'

'More secret. He's part of a very small group, they have to protect the Queen. The other Royals too, but the Queen especially. I'm not supposed to talk about it. Swear you won't tell anyone.'

Rod swore, but of course told his father. Later Lance showed Rod a newspaper photograph of the invasion of Suez, and said one of the background figures was his father.

'Thought you said he was protecting the Queen. What's this got to do with her?'

Lance realised he had made a mistake. 'That isn't all his group does. They've got other duties.'

Rod was a large youth with small eyes and a pig's upturned nose. 'My dad says you're making it all up. Just fairy stories, he says.'

'Your dad doesn't *know*.' But after that Lance gave up the stories about his father, who was becoming more and more absent-minded, withdrawn into what Lance supposed were secret thoughts. In the evening, after supper, he switched on the television and sat staring at it with no apparent awareness of what he was watching.

He received few letters, but one morning a long envelope came, name and address typed. Mr Tennyson examined the postmark, turned over the envelope and looked at the back (Lance thought immediately of secret messages), slit it open, read the contents carefully, pushed aside his cereal, took off his glasses and wiped his eyes, spoke.

'Your mother. She's dead. A car accident. She was on her own. Apparently she'd been drinking.'

Lance felt nothing. It seemed to him an age ago that they had lived in the red brick house with the front and back garden, that Pierre had made shillings come out of his ears, his father had come home on leave and read the *Idylls* to him. A curtain had been dropped in his mind, concealing that world as if it had never existed. Reality was here and now, the little flat where he lived, the school he would soon be leaving, and the secret world in which Judy/Guinevere entered the arms of Lancelot.

'I loved her, you know. In spite of everything I loved her. We were never divorced and I always hoped she would come back. I know it was my fault.' At that Lance was indignant. Esme had left her home and her child, how could it have been her husband's fault? Mr Tennyson shook his head. 'You don't understand, how could you? She was a kind of dream to me, and she didn't like dreamers.' He gave his son what almost seemed a glare through the pebbled glasses. 'What about you? You're leaving at the end of this term, what do you want to do?'

'I don't know. I don't want to go to a university. Something exciting.'

His father's laugh was a rusty caw. 'No money for a university, I can tell you that. Something exciting, that's stupid.'

'What you used to read to me, the *Idylls*, that was exciting.'

'That was reading, poetry. Very nice, but not real. Perhaps I shouldn't have – you must get started, that's the thing. I might be able to help.' For a moment Lance had a vision of his own place in that imaginary world in which his father was an agent, but the next words dispelled it. 'Customs and Excise.'

'What?'

'A Customs officer, good safe job. I'll make enquiries, might be able to pull some strings.'

And the strings were pulled, so that Lance became a member of HM Customs and Excise. There was a training period in which he learned what to look out for, the sort of travellers likely to have watches loaded on both arms, the likely drug stuffers and swallowers, the foolish innocents who thought they could break the rules just this once and showed awareness of it in their faces and gestures.

It sounded exciting, and he imagined scenes in which the secret life became reality. There would be a woman traveller, not exactly beautiful but elegant, stylish, the kind of woman whose very appearance left him tongue-tied. She walked through the 'Nothing to Declare' channel at the airport, cool and faintly disdainful. He asked her to open a case, and her raised eyebrows asked *Can you really mean it?*, but were then replaced by a panic-stricken *I may just have forgotten . . .* And then the opened case revealed – what? Something forgivable, an undeclared item from St Laurent, a small storehouse of scents, something on which she need not be taken to court.

Afterwards she was grateful, asked his name, was enchanted to know it was Lancelot, suggested a meeting – but at that point fantasy was checked, for there were strict rules about such matters and he was not sure that he wanted to break them. In any case the disdainful elegant ladies remained in his imagination. He encountered in his duties instead pathetic Africans or South Americans who carried drugs in stomach or anus, or petty villains who travelled a lot by air on genuine business, and fancied their chances of getting drugs or watches through Customs as a kind of perk. Being a Customs officer at an airport, as he said to his father, was as dull a job as any other.

A few months after Lance began work Mr Tennyson took early retirement from the Ministry. Was the retirement purely voluntary, or had it been urged on him by his superiors? Either way, he showed unmistakable signs of a mental decline that was more than absent-mindedness. He would go out shopping, wander off to a nearby park, sit there for an hour or two and return having forgotten to do the shopping. In the flat he let milk boil over on the stove, forgot to turn off a gas fire so that it burned all night, and almost caused a fire by leaving an electric iron on while watching television. At times he thought Esme was still alive and was coming back to live with them, so that he cleared a cupboard for her clothes and rearranged all the furniture. When Lance first got the Customs and Excise job he thought of looking for an apartment of his own, but it was borne in on him that this was not possible. He would have to look after his father, who although insisting that he was perfectly well (and seeming healthier than when he was at the Ministry) admitted to becoming absent-minded.

Mr Tennyson's interest in the *Idylls* had lapsed after news of Esme's death, but it revived in retirement. He read biographies of Tennyson, and deluged Lance with quotations from the *Idylls,* most of them designed to dampen what he saw as his son's unhealthy yearning for excitement. Life, he said, was a great teacher, and he quoted: 'A young man will be wiser by and by'. Not only a great teacher, Life, but it cut you down to size. 'The dirty nurse, Experience, in her kind hath foul'd me' – Lance should remember that this had happened to his father in the sad loss of his wife. After he had gained experience he should look for a nice girl, and inevitably his father quoted: 'In the spring a young man's fancy . . .'

Brutality was not in Lance's nature, but he came near to it then. 'And what would you do when I found a girl, live with us? My wife might have something to say about that.'

Nothing like that, Mr Tennyson said, adding with insufferable complacency: 'No need to worry, I can look after myself.' The obvious truth was that he couldn't.

But the problem didn't arise, because Elaine the fair maid of Astolat who died for love of Lancelot, and Guinevere whom he loved guiltily, remained as much figures of the secret world as the disdainful woman traveller. Lance found it hard to know what to say to girls. When he looked in the glass a moon face stared back at him with eyes owlish behind the round glasses, and a head that wobbled so much on its thin neck that it seemed likely to fall off. What girl could fancy someone who looked like that?

On the other hand it was true that Rod, who was certainly not handsome, pulled plenty of girls. He chatted them up when they stopped at the stall he had in the local market, where he sold all sorts of odds and ends including stuff bought by his father the scrap merchant. 'Nothing to it,' Rod said, little pig eyes twinkling. 'Couple of drinks, bit of a chat, and bang you're in.'

That was all right perhaps for Rod, who had his own place, but Lance couldn't possibly have shocked his father by taking a girl back to their flat. Rod immediately said go back with him, Lance could have the bedroom, he wasn't fussy, he and his girl would manage on the sitting-room sofa. Got to get your leg over sometime, Rod said, plenty of nookie about, no need to pay prossies for it. The sly sideways glance he gave when saying that was justified. Lance had been with prostitutes. Such encounters at least involved no chatting up, but although as Rod put it he got his leg over, these brief encounters were not satisfying. After them he felt ashamed, for they seemed a betrayal of the tall fair slender girl he met in the secret life, the girl to whom no words had to be spoken, no explanations made. They met, crossed the stile, walked hand in hand towards the darkness of the wood and the brightness of the bluebells that made a carpet within it, and then lay down together.

It was through Rod that the secret life and Lance's everyday world became one. Rod played for a pub darts team, and occasionally Lance went along to watch. Two girls were with Rod, one fair, one dark.

'Del, you know Lance,' Rod said. 'Gwyn, this is Lance I was telling you about, works in Customs. Want to watch out for him, he's a tiger, so they tell me.' General laughter. 'You should see him in his uniform, he's hot stuff.'

'I can imagine,' the dark girl said, not joking, as if she meant it.

Lance bought a round. The dark girl spoke to him. 'Rod was on about you, said you were dead clever only you don't talk much. Why's that?'

'Nothing to say, I expect.'

'Doesn't stop me, Del, does it? You either.' She laughed, showing regular teeth. 'But you, Lance, I bet you're deep. Is he deep, Rod?'

'Deep as the deep blue sea,' Rod said. At this too there was laughter, and Lance did not feel it was directed at him. When the dark girl went on to ask what he was thinking about he said: 'All right, I'll tell you. Your name, Gwyn. Why are you called that, what's it short for?'

'Nosy, aren't we? Okay, I don't mind telling, it's Gwyneth. Gwyneth Lewis, there's Welsh for you. What about Lance, what sort of name is that?'

For once, strangely, he did not mind saying his name was Lancelot, even added that he thought Gwyn might have been short for Guinevere.

'That's King Arthur, I know about him, saw the film. She was Arthur's wife. But then she and Lancelot—' She looked at Lance, burst out laughing.

A couple of hours and more than a couple of drinks later, the darts match lost, Rod said to him at the bar: 'You're well away there, boy, Gwyn fancies you.'

'She does?' Rod closed one little eye. But it still seemed incredible to Lance, and in any case where could he take Gwyn, who was dark instead of fair but still might really be Guinevere? He was not sure he had enough money for a hotel. But that turned out to be no problem at all. When they left the pub she took his arm and said: 'My place, all right?'

What followed was shocking, exciting and exhausting, quite unlike the brief encounters he had known. Just after midnight he remembered his father, said he must telephone.

'You what?'

'I must tell my father. He'll be worried.'

She stared at him, and for a moment he thought she was going to tell him to get out, go home. Instead she put up a hand, stroked his cheek. 'You're funny. Okay, there's the phone.'

His father's voice was first indignant, then petulant. Did Lance know the time, surely he could have rung earlier, where was he, why couldn't he come home? At the end he said Lance was unkind and thoughtless, and put down the telephone without saying goodbye.

In the morning she made toast and coffee, then went back to bed. He asked if she was out of work.

'I'm on and off, and this week's off. I do jobs for a travel agency, escorting groups, mostly Spain and Portugal. Bloody hard work, don't let anyone tell you different. Next week I'm taking some old dears to Amsterdam, coach tour.' She laughed. 'Last time I mislaid one, turned out he'd gone to the casino, won a bagful of money, got beaten up, landed in hospital. They blamed me, wouldn't you know?'

When Lance had dressed he didn't know what he should say. 'Can I—' He began again. 'I mean, I don't suppose you're free—'

'Thought you'd never ask. Free as air, Lance. Funny name, but I like it, reminds me of something, wonder what it can be?'

'What – oh, I see.' He blushed, and she laughed. She did not speak the language of Guinevere, and she was not like the woman who inhabited the secret world, but her face coalesced in the image of the fair-haired Guinevere who knelt at Lancelot's feet.

When he stood in the Customs hall and sat in the canteen the Gwyn who walked beside him in the secret world, who crossed the stile and went down the path with him to the bluebell wood, was Gwyn who had been transformed into Guinevere.

Each evening after work he met her. Twice they went out with Rod and his Delia, but he liked it best when they were on their own. They saw a film, went to a concert, ate in cheap restaurants, and talked – or for the most part Lance talked and she listened, for his diffidence had gone, he had become eloquent, talking of King Arthur and the *Idylls* and Lancelot's love for Guinevere. And they went to bed, about which she was more urgent than he. The physical act offered a kind of fulfilment of his worship of Guinevere, yet something about it seemed to him messy and coarse, unlike love in the secret world. There you kissed and fondled, but there was none of the sticky glueing of mouth to mouth, nor the moans and subdued shrieks that Gwyn uttered, sounds that had no place in a Tennysonian idyll.

After that first night they spent only evenings together. Mr Tennyson grumbled about his late return to the flat, but accepted Lance's explanation about being short-handed and working extra hours, and one of his colleagues at work said he seemed almost human, instead of going through the motions like a robot. Only Gwyn showed dissatisfaction when he left her. 'You don't want to stay, that it?' she asked. Lance said his father, an old man, couldn't be left alone to look after himself. She shook her head.

'You got to look after number one in this world. And have fun. Still, we do that, don't we?' He said yes, although the physical business was something he found increasingly a problem, and having fun was not an adequate description of the joy he had in the secret world which he could create even in the canteen or walking along the street – but most of all in bed alone at night when coarse-speaking Gwyn became sweet

Guinevere. He was transported into that life even in her presence now, so that one evening she tapped his forehead and said: 'Anyone home? Didn't hear, did you? I said next week I can't see you, taking these old dears to Amsterdam. Not that the red light district there will do any of 'em much good.' Her laugh was loud. 'We'll be back Saturday though, I can see you Sunday. Thing is, are you on that weekend?' He said he was.

'I want you to stop me, check my bags.' She went on quickly. 'Tell you for why. My boss is coming on the trip, nosy bastard, one of the other girls has got it in for me, told him I'm bringing in stuff I shouldn't, know what I mean? So my young brother Billy, he wants a watch, I'm going to buy one out there, go through the "Something To Declare" channel, pay the duty, okay?'

'Yes, but I don't see—'

'You look at the rest of my gear, check it, give it the okay, show the little fat bastard that's my boss where he gets off trying to climb into bed with me. Which is all he wants, I may say. I hate fat men, starving lean hungry ones are my meat.' She giggled. 'Just think what Sunday'll be like when I'm back, I'll have been good for a week.'

He hardly missed her physical presence in the week while she was away. She existed in the secret world, transformed into the Guinevere of the *Idylls* by a chaste radiant glow that surrounded her. He imagined her watching him fighting in the tournament, telling him that she loved him even though she knew this love to be a betrayal, but the scene most persistent in his mind was that when they walked along the path to the bluebell wood, and there lay down together in a tree's green shade. It was the world he had so often read about made real, that world

> Where falls not hail, nor rain, or any snow,
> Nor ever wind blows loudly, but it lies
> Deep-meadow'd, happy, fair with orchard lawns
> And bowery hollows crown'd with summer sea.

Mr Tennyson cheered up no end at having his son home every evening, managed some shopping and cooking successfully, and said it was just like old times. The Chief Customs Officer at the airport, on the other hand, said Lance wanted to wake his ideas up, he looked like a tit in a trance, and it was true that as he stood with a couple of other officers, smart in their uniforms, he absented himself from the passengers who streamed past looking happy, eager or anxious, pushing and wheeling bags and cases.

He was absent in the world of Lancelot, or only half-present, when a voice said: 'Got the receipt somewhere,' and he was suddenly aware of Gwyn before him, Gwyn pushing a trolley that held a suitcase and a holdall. She wore a dark blue raincoat and a jaunty blue hat with a red feather in it. Behind her a fellow Customs officer whose carrot-coloured hair had brought him the name Red, mouthed something silently and grinned. There was no sign of the little fat boss, who had perhaps gone through the 'Nothing to Declare' channel with the rest of her party.

Lance looked at the watch she showed him in its case, and at the receipt, got a list to check the duty payable, tapped the case and holdall and asked her to open them.

Gwyn looked at Red in mock despair, he shook his

head sympathetically. She unlocked the case, zipped open the holdall, over-dramatically gave him her handbag, stood back.

Lance's fingers moved lightly among jacket and skirts, underwear, powder, lipstick, scent. He replaced them, and was about to zip up the holdall when beneath his fingertips he felt the hint of an obstacle, nothing more than a rucked-up bit of lining perhaps, except that no lining should have existed there. He looked up to find Gwyn's large dark eyes staring into his own challengingly, expectantly. His fingers moved further, more carefully, over the holdall's surface, and he knew the obstacle was not a natural one.

There was then a moment of uncertainty for him, a moment when Gwyn's lips – could they ever have been Guinevere's? – curved in a confident smile. Then the smile was broken, the whole shape of her face seemed to change and splinter as he picked up her bags and said they would need to examine them more closely. She made for him, claws out and spitting words never used by Guinevere, and Red had to help him restrain her.

The velour-lined false pocket in the holdall contained uncut diamonds, emeralds and sapphires. As Red said wonderingly, it was hard to see why the silly bitch played it the way she did, calling attention to herself over the watch. If she'd gone through the 'Nothing to Declare' channel she'd have had a chance of getting through, though they always took a look at couriers in charge of groups. As it was, Gwyneth Lewis was duly charged, and released on bail.

*

'You're silent tonight,' Mr Tennyson said. 'Something on your mind?'

'Betrayal.'

'What's that? Something from the *Idylls*?'

'Not from the *Idylls*. I'm going out.'

He wandered aimlessly about the streets, found himself outside the pub where he met Gwyn, went in. Rod was at the bar, a glass raised. Beer sprayed from his mouth when he saw Lance. 'You got a nerve,' he said, 'coming in here, showing your face.'

'I don't understand.'

'Gwyn gave it you straight enough, didn't she? Asked you to check her stuff, what you think she did that for? So you could shop her? All you had to do was charge duty on the watch, pass her through, there was a century in it for you. Woulda been more next time. Whatsa matter, more stupid than you look, are you?' Rod's snout was very close to Lance. 'You landed everybody in it, me included for making the intro. And you should look out, she's Corney Barrow's girl.'

Corney Barrow was well known locally, a villain reputed to have a hand in everything from acting as a fence to selling dope. 'You mean—'

'I said I made the intro, Corney wanted an in at the airport, I said you could be useful getting stuff through. Now you dropped his girl in it. You want to watch yourself, mate. If I were you I'd move out of the area for a while.' Lance said that was not possible because of his father. 'Suit yourself,' Rod said, and turned away.

So he had been betrayed by Gwyn, and betrayed her in his turn, because he had been forced to realise she was Gwyneth Lewis and not Guinevere. But as he went from one pub to another, drinking whisky to which he was unused, the image of Gwyn faded and was replaced wholly by that of Guinevere, looking as in the picture so lovingly, so yearningly, at Lancelot. The lustre of her fair hair was with him as he left the last pub, and three of them came out after him. He saw light flash on steel, heard only faintly the voice say something about a present from Corney. There was a pain in his side, a dull but deepening pain, and he felt himself truly Sir Lancelot, suffering as 'a spear prick'd sharply his own cuirass, and the head pierc'd thro' his side, and there snapt, and remain'd'. Lancelot then cried out her name: 'Guinevere,' he cried, 'the flower of all the west and all the world.' He hardly felt what seemed the hoofbeats trampling and kicking him, and in his last moments was aware only that Guinevere had taken his hand and was leading him down to the peace of the bluebell wood where they would rest forever.

A Canticle for Wulfstan

A Sister Fidelma Mystery

Peter Tremayne

A Canticle for Wulfstan

A Sister Fidelma Mystery

Abbot Laisran smiled broadly. He was a short, rotund, red-faced man. His face proclaimed a permanent state of jollity, for he had been born with that rare gift of humour and a sense that the world was there to provide enjoyment to those who inhabited it. When he smiled, it was no faint-hearted parting of the lips but an expression that welled from the depths of his being, bright and all-encompassing. And when he laughed it was as though the whole earth trembled in accompaniment.

'It is so good to see you again, Sister Fidelma,' Laisran boomed and his voice implied it was no mere formula but a genuine expression of his joy in the meeting.

Sister Fidelma answered his smile with an almost urchin grin, quite at odds with her habit and calling.

Indeed, those who examined the young woman closely, observing the rebellious strands of red hair thrusting from beneath her head-dress, seeing the bubbling laughter in her green eyes, and the natural expression of merriment on her fresh, attractive face, would wonder why such an alluring young woman had taken up the life of a religieuse. Her tall, yet well-proportioned figure seemed to express a desire for a more active and joyous role in life than that in the cloistered confines of a religious community.

'And it is good to see you again, Laisran. It is always a pleasure to come to Durrow.'

Abbot Laisran reached out both his hands to take Fidelma's extended one, for they were old friends. Laisran had known Fidelma since she had reached 'the age of choice', and he, it was, who had persuaded her to take up the study of law under the Brehon Morann of Tara. Further, he had persuaded her to continue her studies until she had reached the qualification of *Anruth,* one degree below that of *Ollamh,* the highest rank of learning. It had been Laisran who had advised her to join the community of Brigid at Kildare when she had become accepted as a *dálaigh,* an advocate of the Brehon Court. In the old days, before the Light of Christ reached the shores of Éireann, all those who held professional office were of the caste of Druids. When the Druids gave up their power to the priests and communities of Christ, the professional classes, in turn, enlisted in the new holy orders as they had done in the old.

'Shall you be long among us?' inquired Laisran.

Fidelma shook her head.

'I am on a journey to the shrine of the Blessed Patrick at Ard Macha.'

'Well, you must stay and dine with us this night. It is a long time since I have had a stimulating talk.'

Fidelma grimaced with humour.

'You are abbot of one of the great teaching monasteries of Ireland. Professors of all manner of subjects reside here with students from the four corners of Ireland. How can you be lacking stimulating discourse?'

Laisran chuckled.

'These professors tend to lecture, there is little dialogue. How boring monologues can be. Sometimes I find more intelligence among our students.'

The great monastery on the plain of the oaks, which gave it the name Durrow, was scarcely a century old but already its fame as a university had spread to many peoples of Europe. Students flocked to the scholastic island, in the middle of the Bog of Aillín, from numerous lands. The Blessed Colmcille had founded the community at Durrow before he had been exiled by the High King and left the shores of Éireann to form his more famous community on Iona in the land of the Dàl Riada.

Sister Fidelma fell in step beside the Abbot as he led the way along the great vaulted corridors of the monastery towards his chamber. Brothers and laymen scurried quietly hither and thither through the corridors, heads bowed, intent to their respective classes or devotions. There were four faculties of learning at Durrow, theology, medicine, law and the liberal arts.

It was mid-morning, halfway between the first Angelus bell and the summons of the noonday Angelus. Fidelma had been up before dawn and had travelled fifteen miles to reach Durrow on horseback, the ownership of a horse being a privilege accorded only to her rank as a representative of the Brehon Court.

A solemn-faced monk strode across their path, hesitated and inclined his head. He was a thin, dark-eyed man of swarthy skin who wore a scowl with the same ease that Abbot Laisran wore a smile. Laisran made a curious gesture of acknowledgment with his hand, more as one of dismissal than recognition, and the man moved off into a side room.

'Brother Finan, our professor of law,' explained Laisran, almost apologetically. 'A good man but with no sense of humour at all. I often think he missed his vocation and that he was designed in life to be a professional mourner.'

He cast a mischievous grin at her.

'Finan of Durrow is well respected among the Brehons,' replied Fidelma, trying to keep her face solemn. It was hard to keep a straight face in the company of Laisran.

'Ah,' sighed Laisran, 'it would lighten our world if you came to teach here, Fidelma. Finan teaches the letter of the law, whereas you would explain to our pupils that often the law can be for the guidance of the wise and the obedience of fools, that justice can sometimes transcend law.'

Sister Fidelma bit her lip.

'There is sometimes a moral question which has to be resolved above the law,' she agreed. 'Indeed, I have had to face decisions between law and justice.'

'Exactly so. Finan's students leave here with a good knowledge of the law but often little knowledge of justice. Perhaps you will think on this?'

Sister Fidelma hesitated.

'Perhaps,' she said guardedly.

Laisran smiled and nodded.

'Look around you, Fidelma. Our fame as a centre of learning is even known in Rome. Do you know, no fewer than eighteen languages are spoken among our students? We resort to Latin and sometimes Greek as our lingua franca. Among the students that we have here are not just the children of the Gael. We have a young Frankish prince, Dagobert, and his entourage. There are Saxon princes, Wulfstan, Eadred and Raedwald. Indeed, we have a score of Saxons. There is Talorgen, a prince of Rheged in the land of Britain . . .'

'I hear that the Saxons are making war on Rheged and attempting to destroy it so they can expand their borders,' observed Fidelma. 'That cannot make for easy relationships among the students.'

'Ah, that is so. Our Irish monks in Northumbria attempt to teach these Saxons the ways of Christ, and of learning and piety, but they remain a fierce warrior race intent on conquest, plunder and land. Rheged may well fall like the other kingdoms of the Britons before them. Elmet fell when I was a child. Where the Britons of Elmet once dwelt, now there are Saxon farmers and Saxon thanes.'

They halted before Laisran's chamber door. The Abbot opened it to usher Fidelma inside.

'There has been perpetual warfare between the Britons and the Saxons for the last two-and-a-half centuries,' frowned Fidelma, as she entered. 'Surely it is hard to contain both Briton and Saxon within the same hall of learning?'

They moved into Laisran's official chamber, which he used for administrating the affairs of the great monastery. He motioned Fidelma to be seated before a smouldering turf fire and went to pour wine from an earthenware jug on the table, handing a goblet to her and raising the other in salute.

'*Agimus tibi gratias, Omnipotens Deus,*' he intoned solemnly but with a sparkle of humour in his eyes.

'Amen,' echoed Sister Fidelma, raising the goblet to her lips and tasting the rich red wine of Gaul.

Abbot Laisran settled himself in a chair and stretched out his feet towards the fire.

'Difficult to contain Briton and Saxon?' he mused, after a while. In fact, Sister Fidelma had almost forgotten that she had asked the question. 'Yes. We have had several fights among the Britons and the Saxons here. Only the prohibition of weapons on our sacred ground has so far prevented injury.'

'Why don't you send one group or the other to another centre of learning?'

Laisran sniffed.

'That has already been suggested by Finan, no less. A neat, practical and logical suggestion. The question is . . . which group? Both Britons and Saxons refuse to go, each group demanding that if anyone leave Durrow then it should be the other.'

'Then you have difficulties,' observed Fidelma.

'Yes. Each is quick to anger and slow to forget an insult, real or imaginary. One Saxon princeling, Wulfstan, is very arrogant. He has ten in his retinue. He comes from the land of the South Saxons, one of the smaller Saxon kingdoms but to hear him speak you would think that his kingdom encompassed the world.

The sin of pride greatly afflicts him. After his first clash with the Britons he demanded that he be given a chamber whose window was barred from ingress and whose door could be bolted from the inside.'

'A curious request in a house of God,' agreed Sister Fidelma.

'That is what I told him. But he told me that he feared for his life. In fact, so apprehensive was his manner, so genuine did his fear appear, that I decided to appease his anxiety and provide him with such a chamber. I gave him a room with a barred window in which we used to keep transgressors but had our carpenter fix the lock so that the door could be barred from the inside. Wulfstan is a strange young man. He never moves without a guard of five of his retinue. And after Vespers, he retires to his room, but has his retinue search it before he enters and only then will he enter alone and bar the door. There he remains until the morning Angelus.'

Sister Fidelma pursed her lips and shook her head in wonder.

'Truly one would think him greatly oppressed and frightened. Have you spoken to the Britons?'

'I have, indeed. Talorgen, for example, openly admits that all Saxons are enemies of his blood but that he would not deign to spill Saxon blood in a house of God. In fact, the young Briton rebuked me, saying that his people had been Christian for centuries and had made no war on sacred ground unlike the Saxons. He reminded me that within the memory of living man, scarcely half a century ago, the Saxon warriors of Aethelfrith of Northumbria had defeated Selyf map Cynan of Powys in battle at a place called Caer Legion, but then profaned their victory by slaughtering a thousand British monks from Bangor-is-Coed. He averred that the Saxons were scarcely Christian in thought and barely so in word and deed.'

'In other words . . .?' prompted Fidelma when Laisran paused to sip his wine.

'In other words, Talorgen would not harm a Saxon protected by the sacred soil of a Christian house but he left no doubt that he would not hesitate to slay Wulfstan outside these walls.'

'So much for Christian charity, love and forgiveness,' sighed Fidelma.

'Well,' grimaced Laisran, 'one must remember that the Britons have suffered greatly at the hands of the Saxons during these last centuries. After all, the Saxons have invaded and conquered much of their land. Ireland has received great communities of refugees fleeing from the Saxon conquests in Britain.'

Fidelma smiled whimsically.

'Do I detect that you approve of Talorgen's attitude?'

Laisran grinned.

'If you ask me as a Christian, no; no, of course not. If you ask me as a member of a race who once shared a common origin, belief and law with our cousins, the Britons, then I must say to you that I have a sneaking sympathy for Talorgen's anger.'

There came a sudden banging at the door of the chamber, so loud and abrupt that both Laisran and Fidelma started in surprise. Before the Abbot had time to call out, the door burst open and a middle-aged monk, his face red, his clothes awry from running, burst breathlessly into the room.

He halted a few paces inside the door, his shoulders

heaving, his breath panting from exertion.

Laisran rose, his brows drawing together in an unnatural expression of annoyance.

'What does this mean, Brother Ultan? Have you lost your senses?'

The man shook his head, eyes wide. He gulped air, trying to recover his breath.

'God between us and all evil,' he got out at last. 'There has been a murder committed.'

Laisran's composure was severely shaken.

'Murder, you say?'

'Wulfstan, the Saxon, your grace! He has been stabbed to death in his chamber.'

The blood drained from Laisran's face and he cast a startled glance towards Sister Fidelma. Then he turned back to Brother Ultan, his face now set in stern lines.

'Compose yourself, Brother,' he said kindly, 'and tell me slowly and carefully. What has occurred?'

Brother Ultan swallowed nervously and sought to collect his thoughts.

'Eadred, the companion of Wulfstan, came to me during the mid-morning hour. He was troubled. Wulfstan had not attended the morning prayers nor had he been at his classes. No one had seen him since he retired into his chamber following Vespers last night. Eadred had gone to his chamber and found the door closed. There was no response to his summons at the door. So, as I am master of the household, he came to see me. I accompanied him to Wulfstan's chamber. Sure enough, the door was closed and clearly barred on the inside.'

He paused a moment and then continued.

'Having knocked a while, I then, with Eadred's help,

forced the door. It took a while to do, and I had to summon the aid of two other Brothers to eventually smash the wooden bars that secured it. Inside the chamber . . . ' he bit his lip, his face white with the memory.

'Go on,' ordered Laisran.

'Inside the chamber was the body of Wulfstan. He lay back on the bed. He was in his night attire which was stained red with congealed blood. There were many wounds in his chest and stomach. He had been stabbed several times. It was clear that he had been slain.'

'What then?'

Brother Ultan was now more firmly in control. He contrived to shrug at Laisran's question.

'I left the two Brothers to guard the chamber. I told Eadred to return to his room and not to tell anyone until I sent for him. Then I came immediately to inform you, your grace.'

'Wulfstan killed?' Laisran whispered as he considered the implications. 'Then God protect us, indeed. The land of the South Saxons may be a small kingdom but these Saxons band together against all foreigners. This could lead to some incident between the Saxons and the land of Éireann.'

Sister Fidelma came forward from her seat, frowning at the master of the household.

'Let me get this clear, Brother Ultan, did you say that the chamber door was locked from the inside?'

Brother Ultan examined her with a frown of annoyance, turning back to Abbot Laisran as though to ignore her.

'Sister Fidelma is a *dálaigh* of the Brehon Court, Brother,' Laisran rebuked softly.

The Brother's eyes widened and he turned hurriedly back to Sister Fidelma with a look of respect.

'Yes, the door of Wulfstan's chamber was barred from the inside.'

'And the window was barred?'

A look of understanding crossed Ultan's face.

'No one could have entered or left the chamber through the window, Sister,' he said slowly, swallowing hard as the thought crystallised in his mind.

'And yet no one could have left by the door?' pressed Sister Fidelma remorselessly.

Ultan shook his head.

'Are you sure that the wounds of Wulfstan were not self-inflicted?'

'No!' whispered Ultan, swiftly genuflecting.

'Then how could someone have entered his chamber, slaughtered him and left it, ensuring that the door was bolted from the inside?'

'God help us, Sister!' cried Ultan. 'Whoever did this deed was a sorcerer! An evil demon able to move through walls of stone!'

Abbot Laisran halted uneasily at the end of the corridor in which two of his brethren stood to bar the way against any inquisitive members of the brethren or students. Already, in spite of Brother Ultan's attempt to stop the spread of the news, word of Wulfstan's death was being whispered among the cloisters. Laisran turned to Sister Fidelma who had followed at his heels, calm and composed, her hands now folded demurely in the folds of her gown.

'Are you sure that you wish to undertake this task, Sister?'

Sister Fidelma wrinkled her nose.

'Am I not an advocate of the Brehon Court? Who else should conduct this investigation if not I, Laisran?'

'But the manner of his death . . .'

She grimaced and cut him short.

'I have seen many bodies and only a few have died peacefully. This is the task that I was trained for.'

Laisran sighed and motioned the two Brothers to stand aside.

'This is Sister Fidelma, a *dálaigh* of the Brehon Court who is investigating the death of Wulfstan on my behalf. Make sure that she has every assistance.'

Laisran hesitated, raised his shoulder almost in a gesture of bewilderment, then turned and left.

The two Brothers stood aside respectfully as Sister Fidelma hesitated at the door.

The chamber of Wulfstan was one which led off a corridor of dark granite stone on the ground floor of the monastery. The door, which now hung splintered on its hinges, was thick – perhaps about two inches thick – and had been attached to the door frame with heavy iron hinges. Unlike most doors that she was accustomed to, there was no iron handle on the outside. She paused a while, her keen green eyes searching the timber of the door which showed the scuffing of Ultan's attempts to force it.

Then she took a step forward but stayed at the threshold, letting her keen eyes travel over the room beyond.

Beyond was a bed, a body laid sprawled on its back, arms flung out, head with wild staring eyes glazed towards the ceiling in a last painful gape preceding death. The body was clad in a white shirt which was splattered with blood. The wounds were certainly not self inflicted.

From her position, she saw a small wooden chair, on which was flung a pile of clothes. There was also a small table with an oil lamp and some writing materials on it. There was little else in the room.

The light entered the gloomy chamber from a small window which stood at a height of eight feet from the floor and was criss-crossed with iron bars through which one might thrust an arm to shoulder length, but certainly no more than that could pass beyond. All four walls of the chamber were of stone blocks while the floor as well was flagged in great granite slabs. The ceiling of the room was of dark oak beams. There was little light to observe detail in the chamber, even though it was approaching the noon day. The only light that entered was from the tiny, barred window.

'Bring me a strong lamp, Brothers,' Fidelma called to the two monks in the corridor.

'There is a lamp already in the room, Sister,' replied one of them.

Sister Fidelma hid her annoyance.

'I want nothing in this room touched until I have examined it carefully. Now fetch me the lamp.'

She waited, without moving, until one of the Brothers hurried away and returned with an oil lamp.

'Light it,' instructed Fidelma.

The monk did so.

Fidelma took it from his hand with a nod of thanks.

'Wait outside and let no one into the room until I say so.'

Holding the lamp, she stepped forward into the curious chamber of death.

Wulfstan's throat had been slashed with a knife or sword and there were several great stab wounds in his chest around the heart. His night attire was torn by the weapon and bloodied as were the sheets around him.

On the floor beside the bed was a piece of fine cloth which was bloodstained. The blood had dried. She picked it up and examined it. It was an elegantly woven piece of linen which was embroidered. It carried a Latin motto. She examined the bloodstains on it. It appeared as if whoever had killed Wulfstan had taken the kerchief from his pocket and wiped his weapon clean, letting the kerchief drop to the floor beside the body in a fit of absent-mindedness. Sister Fidelma placed the kerchief in the pocket within the folds of her robe.

She examined the window next. Although it was too high to reach up to it, the bars seemed secure enough. Then she gazed up at the heavy wooden planking and beams which formed the ceiling. It was a high chamber some eleven feet from floor to ceiling. The floor, too, seemed solid enough.

Near the bed she suddenly noticed a pile of ashes. She dropped to one knee beside the ashes and examined them, trying not to disperse them with her breath for they appeared to be the remnants of some piece of paper or vellum perhaps. Not a very big piece either but it was burnt beyond recognition.

She rose and examined the door next.

There were two wooden bars which had secured it. Each bar, when in place, slotted into iron rests. The first was at a height of three feet from the bottom of the door while the second was five feet from the bottom. She saw that one of the iron rests had been splintered from the wooden door jamb, obviously when Ultan had broken in. The pressure against the bar had wrenched the rest from its fastenings. But the bottom set of rests were in place and there was no sign of damage to the second bar which was lying just behind the door. Both bars were solid enough. The ends were wrapped with twine, she presumed to stop the wood wearing against the iron rests in which they lodged. On one of the bars the pieces of twine had become unwound, blackened and frayed at the end.

Sister Fidelma gave a deep sigh.

Here, indeed, was a problem to be solved unless the owner of the kerchief could supply an answer.

She moved to the door and suddenly found herself slipping. She reached out a hand to steady herself. There was a small pool of blackened grease just inside the door. Her sharp eyes caught sight of a similar pool on the other side of the door. Bending to examine them, she frowned as she noticed two nails attached on the door frame, either side of the door. A short length of twine, blackened and frayed at the end, was attached to each nail.

Sister Fidelma compressed her lips thoughtfully and stood staring at the door for a long while before turning to leave the death chamber.

In Abbot Laisran's chamber, Sister Fidelma seated herself at the long table. She had arranged with the Abbot to interview any she felt able to help her in arriving at a solution to the problem. Laisran himself offered to sit in on her encounters but she had felt it unnecessary. Laisran had taken himself to a side room, having presented her with a bell to summon him if she needed any help.

Brother Ultan was recruited to fetch those whom she wanted to see and was straightaway dispatched to bring Wulfstan's fellow Saxon prince, Eadred, who had helped Ultan discover the body, as well as his cousin, Raedwald.

Eadred was a haughty youth with flaxen hair and cold blue eyes that seemed to have little expression. His features seemed fixed with a mixture of disdain and boredom. He entered the chamber, eyes narrowing as he beheld Sister Fidelma. A tall, muscular young man in his late twenties accompanied Eadred. Although he carried no arms, he acted as if he were the prince's bodyguard.

'Are you Eadred?' Fidelma asked the youth.

The young man scowled.

'I do not answer questions from a woman.' His voice was harsh and that combined with his guttural accent made his stilted Irish sound raucous.

Sister Fidelma sighed. She had heard that Saxons could be arrogant and that they treated their womenfolk more as chattels than as human beings.

'I am investigating the death of your countryman, Wulfstan. I need my questions to be answered,' she replied firmly.

Eadred merely ignored her.

'Lady,' it was the tall muscular Saxon who spoke and his knowledge of Irish was better than that of his prince. 'I am Raedwald, thane of Staeningum, cousin to the thane of Andredswald. It is not the custom of princes of our race to discourse with women if they be not of equal royal rank.'

'Then I am obliged for your courtesy in explaining your customs, Raedwald. Eadred, your cousin, seems to lack a knowledge of the law and customs of the country in which he is now a guest.'

Ignoring the angry frown on Eadred's features, she reached forward and rang the silver bell on the table before her. The Abbot Laisran entered from a side room.

'As you warned me, your grace, the Saxons seem to think that they are above the law of this land. Perhaps they will accept the explanation from your lips.'

Laisran nodded and turned to the young men. He bluntly told them of Fidelma's rank and position in law, that even the High King had to take note of her wisdom and learning. Eadred continued to scowl but he inclined his head stiffly when Laisran told him that he was under legal obligation to answer Fidelma's questions. Raedwald seemed to accept the explanation as a matter of course.

'As your countryman considers you of royal rank, I will deign to answer your questions,' Eadred said, moving forward and seating himself without waiting for Fidelma's permission. Raedwald continued to stand.

Fidelma exchanged a glance with Laisran who shrugged.

'The customs of the Saxons are not our customs, Sister Fidelma,' Laisran said apologetically. 'You will ignore their tendency to boorish behaviour.'

Eadred flushed angrily.

'I am a prince of the blood royal of the South Saxons, descended through the blood of Aelle from the great god Woden!'

Raedwald, who stood with folded arms, silently behind him, looked unhappy, opened his mouth and then closed it firmly.

Abbot Laisran genuflected. Sister Fidelma merely

stared at the young man in amusement.

'So you are not yet truly Christian, believing only in the One True God?'

Eadred bit his lip.

'All Saxon royal houses trace their blood-line to Woden, whether god, man or hero,' he responded, with a slightly defensive tone.

'Tell me something of yourself then. I understand that you were cousin to Wulfstan? If you find speaking in our language difficult, you may speak in Latin or Greek. I am fluent in their usage.'

'I am not,' rasped Eadred. 'I speak your language from my study here but I speak no other tongue fluently, though I have some knowledge of Latin.'

Sister Fidelma hid her surprise and gestured for him to continue. Most Irish princes and chieftains she knew spoke several languages fluently besides their own, especially Latin and some Greek.

'Very well. Wulfstan was your cousin, wasn't he?'

'Wulfstan's father Cissa, king of the South Saxons, was brother to my father, Cymen. I am thane of Andredswald as my father was before me.'

'Tell me how Wulfstan and yourself came to be here, in Durrow.'

Eadred sniffed.

'Some years ago, one of your race, a man called Diciul, arrived in our country and began to preach of his god, a god with no name who had a son named Christ. Cissa, the king, was converted to this new god and turned away from Woden. The man of Éireann was allowed to form a community, a monastery, at Bosa's Ham, in our land, and many went to hear him teach. Cissa decided that Wulfstan, who is heir apparent to the kingship, should come to the land of Éireann for education.'

Sister Fidelma nodded wondering whether it was the young man's poor usage of Irish that made him seem so disapproving of Cissa's conversion to Christ.

'Then Wulfstan is the Tanist in your land?'

Abbot Laisran intervened with a smile.

'The Saxons have a different law system to us, Sister Fidelma,' he interrupted. 'They hold that the eldest son inherits all. There is no election by the *derbhfine* such as we have.'

'I see,' nodded Fidelma. 'Go on, Eadred. Cissa decided to send Wulfstan here.'

The young man grimaced sourly.

'I was ordered to accompany him and learn with him. We came together with our cousin Raedwald, thane of Staeningum, together with ten churls and five slaves to attend our needs and here we have been now for six moons.'

'And not the best of our students,' muttered Laisran.

'That's as may be,' snapped Eadred. 'We did not ask to come but were ordered by Cissa. I shall be pleased to depart now and take the body of my kinsman back to my country.'

'Does the Latin inscription "*cave quid dicis*" mean anything to you?'

Eadred sniffed.

'It is the motto of the young Frankish prince, Dagobert.'

Sister Fidelma gazed thoughtfully at the young man before turning to Raedwald. The muscular young man's face was flushed and confused.

'And you, Raedwald? Does it mean anything to you?'

'Alas, I have no Latin, lady,' he mumbled.

'So? And when did you last see Wulfstan?'

'Just after Vespers.'

'What happened exactly?'

'As usual, Wulfstan was accompanied by myself and Eadred, with two of our churls and two slaves, to his chamber for the night. We searched the chamber as usual and then Wulfstan entered and dismissed us.'

Eadred nodded in agreement.

'I talked a while with Raedwald in the corridor. We both heard Wulfstan secure the wooden bars. Then I went off to my chamber.'

Sister Fidelma glanced again towards Raedwald.

'And you can confirm this, Raedwald?'

Eadred flushed.

'You doubt my word?' His voice was brittle.

'This investigation will be conducted under our law, Eadred,' retorted Fidelma in annoyance.

Raedwald looked awkward.

'I can confirm what Eadred says, lady,' he replied. 'The thane of Andredswald speaks the truth. As soon as we heard the bars slide shut we both knew that the prince, Wulfstan, had secured himself in for the night and so we both departed for our sleeping chambers.'

Sister Fidelma nodded thoughtfully.

'You can also confirm, Eadred, that Wulfstan was afraid of being attacked? Why was that?'

Eadred sniffed.

'There are too many mad *welisc* in this place and one in particular had made several threats against him . . . that barbarian Talorgen!'

'*Welisc*? Who are they?' frowned Fidelma, puzzled.

Laisran gave a tired smile.

'The Saxons call all Britons *welisc*. It is a name which signifies that they are foreigners.'

'I see. So you left Wulfstan safely secured in his room? You did not seem to be as afraid of the Britons as your cousin. Why was that?'

Eadred laughed bitterly.

'I would not be thane of Andredswald if I could not defend myself against a pack of *welisc* cowards. No, I fear no barbarian's whelp nor his sire, either.'

'And the rest of your Saxon entourage? Did they fear the Britons?'

'Whether they feared or not, it is of no significance. I command them and they will do as I tell them.'

Sister Fidelma exhaled in exasperation. It would be difficult to live in a Saxon country if one was not a king or a thane, she thought.

'When did you realise that Wulfstan was missing?' she prompted.

'At prayers following the first bell . . .'

'He means the Angelus,' explained Laisran.

'He did not come to prayers and, thinking he had slept late, I went to classes.'

'What classes were these?'

'That weasel-faced Finan's class on the conduct of law between kingdoms.'

'Go on.'

'During the mid-morning break, having realised that Wulfstan was missing, I went to his room. The door was shut, signifying he was still inside. I banged upon the door. There was no response. I then went to look for Brother Ultan, the house-churl . . .'

'The steward of our community,' corrected Laisran softly.

'We went to Wulfstan's chamber and Ultan had to call upon two other Brothers to help us break in the door. Wulfstan had been feloniously slain. One doesn't have to search far for the culprit.'

'And who might that be?' invited Sister Fidelma.

'Why, it is obvious. The *welisc*-man, Talorgen, who calls himself a prince of Rheged. He has threatened Wulfstan's life. And it is well known the *welisc* practise sorcery . . .'

'What do you mean?' Fidelma asked sharply.

'Why, the fact that Wulfstan had been slaughtered in his bed chamber while the window was barred and the door shut and secured from the inside. Who else but a *welisc* would be able to shape-change and perpetrate such a monstrous deed?'

Sister Fidelma hid her cynical smile.

'Eadred, I think you have much to learn for you seem to be wallowing in the superstition of your old religion.'

Eadred sprang up, his hand going to his belt where a knife might be worn.

'I am thane of Andredswald! I consented to be questioned by a mere woman because it is the custom of this land. However, I will not be insulted by one.'

'I am sorry that you think that I insult you,' Sister Fidelma replied, with a dangerous glint in her eyes. 'You may go.'

Eadred's face was working in a rage but Laisran moved forward and opened the door.

The young Saxon prince turned and stormed out. Raedwald hesitated a moment, made a gesture almost of apology and then followed the prince out of the room.

'Did I not tell you that these Saxons are strange,

haughty people, Fidelma?' smiled Laisran almost sadly.

Sister Fidelma shook her head.

'They probably have their good and bad like all peoples. Raedwald seems filled more with the courtesy of princes than his cousin Eadred.'

'Well, if Eadred and his followers are to be judged, then we have had their bad. As for Raedwald, although a thane and older than either Wulfstan or Eadred, he seems quiet and was dominated by them both. He is more of a servant than a master. I gather this is because his cousins both stand in closer relationship to their king than he does.' Laisran paused and cast her a curious glance. 'Why did you ask them about the Latin motto – *cave quid dicis*?'

'It was a motto found on a piece of linen which wiped the weapon that killed Wulfstan. It could have been dropped by the killer or it could have been Wulfstan's.'

Laisran shook his head.

'No. Eadred was right. That belligerent motto, Fidelma, "beware what you say", is the motto of the Frankish prince – Dagobert. I have recently remarked on its pugnacity to the young man.'

Sister Fidelma stretched reflectively. 'It seems things do not look good for Dagobert of the Franks. He now stands as the most likely suspect.'

'Not necessarily. Anyone could have taken and dropped the cloth and there are many here who have come to hate the arrogance of the Saxons. Why, I have even heard the dour Finan declare that he would like to drown the lot of them!'

Fidelma raised her eyebrows.

'Are you telling me that we must suspect Finan, the professor of your law faculty?'

Abbot Laisran suddenly laughed.

'Oh, the idea of Finan being able to shape-change to enter a locked room, commit murder, and sneak out without disturbing the locks is an idea I find amusing but hardly worthy of consideration.'

Sister Fidelma gazed thoughtfully at Laisran.

'Do you believe that this murder could only be carried out by sorcery, then?'

Laisran's rotund face clouded and he genuflected quickly.

'God between me and all evil, Fidelma, but is there any other explanation? We come from a culture which accepted shape-changing as a normal occurrence. Move among our people and they will tell you that druids still exist and have such capabilities. Wasn't Diarmuid's foster brother changed into a boar, and wasn't Caer, the beloved of Aengus Og, condemned to change her form every alternate year?'

'These are ancient legends, Laisran,' admonished Sister Fidelma. 'We live in reality, in the here and now. And it is among the people of this community that we will find the person who slew Wulfstan. Before I question Dagobert, however, I would like to see Wulfstan's chamber once more.'

Abbot Laisran pulled at his lower lip. His usually jovial face was creased in a frown of perplexity.

'I do not understand, Sister Fidelma. Everyone in our community here, at Durrow, had cause to kill Wulfstan and everyone is suspect. Is that what you are saying? At the same time that everyone is suspect, no one could have done the deed for its implementation was beyond the hand of any human agency.'

'Now that I did not say,' Sister Fidelma admonished

the Abbot firmly, as she led the way along the corridor to halt at the open door of what had been Wulfstan's chamber.

The body of Wulfstan had been removed to the chapel of St Benignus where preparations were being made to transport its sarcophagus to the coast, from where Eadred and his entourage would accompany it, by sea, to the land of the South Saxons which lay on the southern shore of Britain.

Sister Fidelma stared once again at the grey stone-flagged floor. She walked over the slabs, pressing each with her foot. Then she stared upwards towards the ceiling which rose about eleven feet above the chamber floor. Her eyes eventually turned back to the bars on the window.

'Give me a hand,' she suddenly demanded.

Abbot Laisran stared at her in surprise as she began pushing the wooden table towards the window.

Hastily, he joined her in the effort, grinning sheepishly.

'If the young novitiates of my order could see their abbot heaving furniture about . . . ' he began.

'They would realise that their abbot was merely human,' replied Fidelma, smiling.

They pushed the table under the barred window and, to Abbot Laisran's astonishment, Sister Fidelma suddenly scrambled on top of the table. It rose three feet above the ground and by standing on it, Sister Fidelma, being tall, could reach easily to the bars of the solitary window whose bottom level was eight feet above the floor. She reached up with both her hands and tested each inch-thick iron bar carefully.

The lowering of her shoulders showed her disappointment.

Slowly she clambered down helped by the arm of Laisran.

Her lips were compressed. 'I thought the bars might have been loose.'

'It was a good idea,' smiled Laisran, encouragingly.

'Come, show me the floor above this,' Sister Fidelma said abruptly.

With a sigh, Laisran hastened after her as she strode swiftly away.

The floor above turned out to be equally disappointing. Over Wulfstan's chamber stretched a long wooden floor which was the floor of one of the long dormitories for the novitiates of the community. There were over a dozen beds in the dormitory. Had Sister Fidelma not examined the boards of the floor carefully, to see whether any had been prised up in order that a person could be lowered into the chamber below, and realised that none of the floorboards had been moved in many years, she would also have realised the fact that such an exercise would have necessitated the participation of everyone in the dormitory.

She turned away with disappointment on her features.

'Tell me, Laisran, what lies below Wulfstan's chamber?'

Laisran shook his head.

'I have had that thought also, Fidelma,' he confided. 'Nothing but solid earth lies below. There is no cellar, nor tunnel. The stone flags are laid on solid ground, so no person could enter the chamber by removing one of the floor stones. Besides,' he smiled wryly, 'what would Wulfstan have been doing during the commotion required to enter his chamber by the removing of the ceiling planks, or floor slabs or the removal of the bars of the window?'

Sister Fidelma smiled.

'The pursuit of truth is paved by the consideration and rejection of all the alternatives, no matter how unlikely they may be, Laisran.'

'The truth,' replied the abbot, looking troubled, 'is that it was impossible for the hand of man to strike down Wulfstan while he was locked alone in his chamber.'

'Now that I *can* agree with.'

Abbot Laisran looked puzzled.

'I thought you said that no sorcery was employed. Do you mean that he was not killed by the hand of man?'

'No,' grinned Sister Fidelma. 'I mean that he was not alone in his chamber. It is a syllogism. Wulfstan was stabbed to death. Wulfstan was in his bedchamber. Therefore he was not alone in his bedchamber when he was killed.'

'But . . .'

'We have ruled out the argument that our murderer could have come through the window. Do you agree?'

Laisran frowned, trying hard to follow the logic.

'We have ruled out the possibility that our murderer could have entered the chamber through the roof.'

'Agreed.'

'We have concluded that it would be impossible for the murderer to enter via the stone flagged floor.'

Abbot Laisran nodded emphatically.

'Then that leaves one obvious method of entry and exit.'

Now Laisran was truly bewildered.

'I do not see . . . ' he began.

'The chamber door. That is how our murderer gained entry and how he left.'

'Impossible!' Laisran shook his head. 'The door was secured from the inside.'

'Nevertheless, that was how it was done. And whoever did it hoped that we would be so bemused by this curiosity that we would not inquire too deeply of the motive, for he hoped the motive was one that was obvious to all. The hatred of Wulfstan and the Saxons. Ideas of sorcery, of evil spirits, of Wulfstan being slain by no human hand, might cloud our judgment, or so our killer desired it to do.'

'Then you know who the killer is?'

Fidelma shook her head.

'I have not questioned all the suspects. I think it is now time that we spoke with the Frankish prince, Dagobert.'

Dagobert was a young man who had been brought from the land of the Franks when he had been a child. It was claimed that he was heir to the Frankish empire but his father had been deposed and the young prince had been taken into exile in Ireland until the time came when he could return. He was tall, dark, rather attractive, and spoke Irish almost as fluently as a native prince. Laisran had warned Sister Fidelma that the young man was well-connected and betrothed to a princess of the kings of Cashel. There would be repercussions if Dagobert was not accorded the full letter of the Brehon Law.

'You know why you are here?' began Sister Fidelma.

'That I do,' the young man smiled. 'The Saxon pig, Wulfstan, has been slain. Outside the band of Saxons who followed the young whelp, there is a smile on the face of every student in Durrow. Does that surprise you, Sister Fidelma?'

'Perhaps not. I am told that you were known to have had an argument with him?'

Dagobert nodded.

'What about?'

'He was an arrogant pig. He insulted my ancestry and so I punched him on the nose.'

'Wasn't that difficult to do, with his bodyguard? I am also told that Raedwald was never far away and he is a muscular young man.'

Dagobert chuckled.

'Raedwald knew when to defend his prince and when not. He diplomatically left the room when the argument started. A man with a sense of honour is Raedwald of the South Saxons. Wulfstan treated him like dirt beneath his feet even though he was a thane and blood cousin.'

Sister Fidelma reached into her robes and drew out the bloodstained embroidered linen kerchief and laid it on the table.

'Do you recognise this, Dagobert?'

Dagobert frowned and picked it up turning it over in his hands with a puzzled expression.

'It is certainly mine. There is my motto. But the bloodstains. . .?'

'It was found by the side of Wulfstan's body. I found it. It was obviously used to wipe the blood off the weapon that killed him.'

Dagobert's face whitened.

'I did not kill Wulfstan. He was a pig but he simply needed a sound thrashing to teach him manners.'

'Then how came this kerchief to be by his side in his chamber?'

'I . . . I loaned it to someone.'

'Who?'

Dagobert bit his lip, shrugging.

'Unless you wish to be blamed for this crime, Dagobert, you must tell me,' insisted Fidelma.

'Two days ago I loaned the kerchief to Talorgen, the prince of Rheged.'

Finan inclined his head to Sister Fidelma.

'Your reputation as an advocate of the Brehon Court precedes you, Sister,' the dark, lean man greeted her. 'Already it is whispered from Tara how you solved a plot to overthrow the High King.'

Fidelma gestured Finan to be seated.

'People sometimes exaggerate another's prowess for they love to create heroes and heroines to worship. You are professor of law here?'

'That is so. I am qualified to the level of *Sai*, being a professor of law only.'

The *Sai* was a qualification of six years of study and the degree below that of *Anruth* held by Fidelma.

'And you taught Wulfstan?'

'Each of us has a cross to bear, as did Christ. Mine was the teaching of the Saxon thanes.'

'Not all the Saxons?'

Finan shook his head.

'No. Only the three thanes as they refused to sit at lessons with churls and only the express order of the Abbot Laisran made them attend class with the other students. They were not humble before the altar of Christ. In fact, I formed the opinion that they secretly mocked Christ and clung to the worship of their outlandish god Woden.'

'You disliked the Saxons?'

'I hated them!'

The vehemence in the man's voice made Sister Fidelma raise her eyebrows.

'Isn't hate an emotion unknown to a Brother of the order, especially one qualified as a *Sai*?'

'My sister and brother took up the robes of the religious and decided to accept a mission to preach the word of Christ in the lands of the East Saxons. A few years ago I encountered one of the missionaries who had gone in that band. They had arrived in the land of the East Saxons and sought to preach the word of Christ. The heathen Saxons stoned them to death, only two of the band escaping. Among those who met a martyr's fate were my own sister and brother. I have hated all Saxons ever since.'

Sister Fidelma gazed into the dark eyes of Finan.

'Did you kill Wulfstan?'

Finan returned her scrutiny squarely.

'I could have done so at another time, in another place. I have the hatred in me. But no, Sister Fidelma, I did not kill him. Neither do I have the means to enter a barred room and leave it as though no one had entered.'

Fidelma nodded slowly.

'You may go, Finan.'

The professor of law rose reluctantly. He paused and said reflectively, 'Wulfstan and Eadred were not liked by any in this monastery. Many young men with hot tempers have challenged them in combat since they have been here. Dagobert the Frank, for one. Only the fact that such challenges are forbidden on sacred soil has prevented bloodshed thus far.'

Fidelma nodded absently.

'Is it true that the Saxons are leaving tomorrow?' Finan demanded.

She raised her head to look at him.

'They are returning with the body of Wulfstan back to their own land,' she affirmed.

A contented smile crossed Finan's face.

'I cannot pretend that I regret that, even if it has cost one of their lives to prompt the move. I had hoped that they would have left Durrow yesterday.'

She glanced up at the law professor, interested.

'Why would they leave?'

'Some Saxon messenger arrived at the monastery yesterday afternoon seeking Wulfstan and Eadred. I half-hoped that it was a summons to return to their country. However, praise be that they are departing now.'

Fidelma frowned in annoyance.

'Let me remind you, Finan, that unless we find the culprit, not only this centre of learning, but all the five kingdoms of Éireann will be at risk for the Saxons will surely want to take compensation for the death of their prince.'

Talorgen of Rheged was a youth of average stature, fresh faced and sandy of hair. He already wore a wispy moustache but his cheeks and chin were clean shaven.

'Yes. It is no secret that I challenged Wulfstan and Eadred to combat.'

His Irish, though accented, was fluent and he seemed at ease as he sat in the chair which Sister Fidelma indicated.

'Why?'

Talorgen grinned impishly.

'I hear that you have questioned Eadred. From his manner you may judge Wulfstan's arrogance. It is not hard to be provoked by them, even if they were not Saxons.'

'You do not like Saxons?'

'They are not likeable.'

'But you are a prince of Rheged, and it is reported that the Saxons are attacking your land.'

Talorgen nodded, his mouth pinched.

'Oswy calls himself Christian king of Northumbria, but he still sends his barbaric hordes against the kingdoms of the Britons. For generations now the people of my land have fought to hold back the Saxons, for their thirst for land and power is great. Owain, my father, sent me here but I would, by the living Christ, rather be at his side, wielding my sword against the Saxon foemen. My blade should drink the blood of the enemies of my blood.'

Sister Fidelma regarded the flushed-faced young man with curiosity.

'Has your blade already drunk of the blood of your people's enemies?'

Talorgen frowned abruptly, hesitating and then his face relaxed. He chuckled.

'You mean, did I kill Wulfstan? That I did not. I swear by the living God! But hear me, Sister Fidelma, it is not that I did not want to. Truly, sometimes the faith of Christ is a hard taskmaster. Wulfstan and his cousin Eadred were so dislikeable that I scarcely believe there is anyone in this community who regrets the death of Wulfstan.'

She took out the bloodstained kerchief and laid it on the table.

'This was found by the body of Wulfstan. It was used to wipe the blood from the weapon that killed him. It belongs to Dagobert.'

'You mean Dagobert . . .?' The prince of Rheged's eyes opened wide as he stared from the kerchief to Sister Fidelma.

'Dagobert tells me that he gave you this kerchief in loan two days ago.'

Talorgen examined the kerchief carefully and then slowly nodded.

'He is right. It is the same one, I can tell from the embroidery.'

'How then did it get into Wulfstan's chamber?'

Talorgen shrugged.

'That I do not know. I remember having it in my chamber yesterday morning. I saw it was gone and thought Dagobert had collected it.'

Sister Fidelma regarded Talorgen steadily for a moment or two.

'I swear, Sister,' said the prince of Rheged earnestly, 'I would not have hesitated to kill Wulfstan outside these walls but I did not kill him within them.'

'You are forthright, Talorgen.'

The young man shrugged.

'I am sprang of the house of Urien of Rheged, whose praise was sung by our great bard Taliesin. Urien was the Golden King of the North, slain in stealth by a traitor. Our house is even-handed, just and forthright. We believe in honesty. We meet our enemies in daylight on the plain of battle, not at night in the darkened recesses of some bedchamber.'

'You say that there are many others in this community who held enmity against Wulfstan? Was there anyone in particular that you had in mind?'

Talorgen pursed his lips.

'Our teacher Finan often told us that he hated the Saxons.'

Sister Fidelma nodded.

'I have spoken with Finan.'

'As you already know, Dagobert quarrelled with Wulfstan in the refectory and bloodied his mouth two nights ago. Then there was Riderch of Dumnonia, Fergna of Midhe and . . .'

Sister Fidelma held up her hand.

'I think that you have made your point, Talorgen. Everyone in Durrow is a suspect.'

Sister Fidelma found Raedwald in the stables making preparations for the journey back to the land of the South Saxons.

'There is a question I would ask you on your own, Raedwald. Need I remind you of my authority?'

The Saxon warrior shook his head.

'I have learnt much of your law and customs since I have been in your country, Sister. I am not as Eadred.'

'And you have learnt some fluency in our tongue,' observed Fidelma. 'More fluency and understanding than your cousin.'

'It is not my place to criticise the heir apparent to the kingship of the South Saxons.'

'But I think that you did not like your cousin Wulfstan?'

Raedwald blinked in surprise at her directness and then he shrugged.

'I am merely a thane in the house of Cissa. I cannot like or dislike my appointed king.'

'Why were you not on guard outside the chamber of Wulfstan last night?'

'It was not the custom. Once Wulfstan had secured himself inside, he was well guarded. You have seen the chamber he asked Abbot Laisran to devise for him. Once he was locked inside, there was, apparently, no danger to him. I slept in the next chamber and at his call should he need help.'

'But he did not call?'

'His killer slashed his throat with his first blow. That much was obvious from his body.'

'It becomes obvious that he willingly let the killer into his chamber. Therefore, he knew the killer and trusted him.'

Raedwald's eyes narrowed.

Fidelma continued.

'Tell me, the messenger who arrived from your country yesterday, what message did he bring Wulfstan?'

Raedwald shook his head.

'That message was for Wulfstan only.'

'Is the messenger still here?'

'Yes.'

'Then I would question him.'

'You may question but he will not answer you,' Raedwald smiled grimly.

Sister Fidelma compressed her lips in annoyance.

'Another Saxon custom? Not even your messengers will speak with women?'

'Another Saxon custom; yes. But this is a custom of kings. The royal messenger has his tongue cut out so that he can never verbally betray the message that he carries from kings and princes to those who might be their enemies.'

Abbot Laisran gestured to those he had summoned to his study chamber, at Sister Fidelma's request, to be seated. They had entered the room with expressions either of curiosity or defiance, according to their different personalities, as they saw Sister Fidelma standing before the high-mantled hearth. She seemed absorbed in her own thoughts as she stood, hands folded demurely before her, not apparently noticing them as they seated themselves around. Brother Ultan, as steward of the community, took his stand before the door with hands folded into his habit.

Abbot Laisran gave Fidelma an anxious glance and then he, too, took his seat.

'Why are we here?' demanded Talorgen abruptly.

Fidelma raised her head to return his gaze.

'You are here to learn how Wulfstan died and by whose hand,' she replied sharply.

There was a brief pause before Eadred turned to her with a sneer.

'We already know how my kinsman Wulfstan died, woman. He died by the sorcery of a barbarian. Who that barbarian is, it is not hard to deduce. It was one of the *welisc* savages, Talorgen.'

Talorgen was on his feet, fists clenched.

'Repeat your charges outside the walls of this abbey and I will meet your steel with mine, Saxon cur!'

Dagobert came to his feet to intervene as Eadred launched forward from his chair towards Talorgen.

'Stop this!' The usually genial features of Laisran

were dark with anger. His voice cut the air like a lash.

The students of the ecclesiastical school of Durrow seemed to freeze at the sound. Then Eadred relaxed and dropped back in his seat with a smile that was more a sneer than amusement. Dagobert tugged at Talorgen's arm and the prince of Rheged sighed and reseated himself as did the Frankish prince.

Abbot Laisran growled like an angry bear.

'Sister Fidelma is an official of the Brehon Court of Éireann. Whatever the customs in your own lands, in this land she has supreme authority in conducting this investigation and the full backing of the law of this kingdom. Do I make myself clear?'

There was a silence.

'I shall continue,' said Fidelma quietly. 'Yet what Eadred says is partially true.'

Eadred stared at her with bewilderment clouding his eyes.

'Oh yes,' smiled Fidelma. '*One* of you at least knows how Wulfstan died and who is responsible.'

She paused to let her words sink in.

'Let me first tell you how he died.'

'He was stabbed to death in his bed,' Finan, the dark-faced professor of law, pointed out.

'That is true,' agreed Sister Fidelma, 'but without the aid of sorcery.'

'How else did the assassin enter a locked room and leave it, still locked from the inside?' demanded Eadred. 'How else but sorcery?'

'The killer wanted us to think that it was sorcery. Indeed, the killer prepared an elaborate plan to confuse us and lay the blame away from him. In fact, so elaborate was the plan that it had several layers. One layer was merely to confuse and frighten us by causing us to think the murder was done by a supernatural agency; another was to indicate an obvious suspect while a third object was to implicate another person.'

'Well,' Laisran sighed, 'at the moment I have yet to see through the first layer.'

Sister Fidelma smiled briefly at the rotund Abbot.

'I will leave that to later. Let us firstly consider the method of the killing.'

She had their complete attention now.

'The assassin entered the room by the door. In fact, Wulfstan let his assassin into the bed chamber himself.'

There was an intake of breath from the usually taciturn Raedwald.

Unperturbed she continued.

'Wulfstan knew his killer. Indeed, he had no suspicions, no fear of this man.'

Abbot Laisran regarded her with open-mouthed astonishment.

'Wulfstan let the killer in,' she continued. 'The assassin struck. He killed Wulfstan and left his body on the bed. It was an act of swiftness. To spread suspicion, the killer wiped his knife on a linen kerchief which he mistakenly thought belonged to Talorgen, prince of Rheged. As I said, if we managed to see beyond the charade of sorcery, then the assassin sought to put the blame for the murder on Talorgen. He failed to realise that the kerchief was borrowed two days ago from Dagobert. He did not realise that the kerchief prominently carried his motto on it. It was a Latin motto which exhorts "beware what you say"!'

She paused to let them digest this information.

'How then did the killer now leave the bed chamber

and manage to bar the door from the inside?' asked Dagobert.

'The bed chamber door was barred with two wooden bars. They were usually placed on iron rests which are attached to the frame of the door. When I examined the first wooden bar I observed that at either end there were two pieces of twine wrapped around it as if to protect the wood when it is placed in the iron rests. Yet on the second wooden bar, the curiosity was that the twine had two lengths of four feet still loose. Each end of the twine had been frayed and charred.'

She grimaced and repeated herself.

'A curiosity. Then I noticed that there was a rail at the top of the door on which a heavy woollen curtain could be drawn across the door when closed in order to prevent a draught. It was, of course, impossible to see whether the curtain had been drawn or not once the room was broken into for the inward movement of the door would have swept the curtain aside on its rail.'

Eadred made a gesture of impatience.

'Where is this explanation leading?'

'Patience and I will tell you. I spotted two small spots of grease on the ground on either side of the door. As I bent to examine these spots of grease I saw two nails fixed into the wood about three inches from the ground. There were two short pieces of twine still tied on these nails and the ends were frayed and blackened. It was then I realised just how the assassin had left the room and left one of the bars in place.'

'One?' demanded Abbot Laisran, leaning forward on his seat, his face eager.

Fidelma nodded.

'Only one was really needed to secure the door from

the inside. The first bar, that at three feet from the bottom of the door, had not been set in place. There were no marks on the bar and its twine protection was intact, nor had the iron rests been wrenched away from the door jamb when Ultan forced the door. Therefore, the conclusion was that this bar was not in place. Only the second bar, that which rested across the top of the door, about two feet from the top, had been in place.'

'Go on,' instructed Laisran when she paused again.

'Having killed Wulfstan, the assassin was already prepared. He undid the twine on both ends of the wooden bar and threaded it around the wood curtain rail across the top of the door. He set in place, or had already placed them during the day when the chamber was open, two nails. Then he raised the wood bar to the level of the curtain rail. He secured it there by tying the ends of the twine to the nails at ground level. This construction allowed him to leave the room.'

Laisran gestured with impatience.

'Yes, but how could he have manipulated the twine to lower the bar in place?'

'Simply. He took two reed candles as he went to leave, he placed a candle under either piece of the string near the ground. He took a piece of paper and lit it from his tinder box – I found the ashes of the paper on the floor of the chamber, where he had to drop it. He lit the two reed candles, on either side of the door under the twine. Then he left quickly. The twine eventually burned through, releasing the bar which dropped neatly into place in the iron rests. It had, remember, only two feet to drop. The candles continued to burn until they became mere spots of grease, almost unnoticeable, except I slipped on one. But the result was that we were left with a mystery. A room locked on the inside with a corpse. Sorcery? No. Planning by a devious mind.'

'So what happened then?' Talorgen encouraged, breaking the spellbound silence.

'The assassin left the room, as I have described. He wanted to create this illusion of mystery because, in his mind, the person he wished to implicate was one he felt his countrymen would believe to be a barbaric sorcerer. As I indicated, he wished to place suspicion on you, Talorgen. He left the room and talked to someone outside Wulfstan's bedchamber for a while. Then they heard the bar drop into place and that was the assassin's alibi, because it was clear that they had heard Wulfstan, still alive, slide the bar to lock his chamber door.'

Raedwald was frowning as it seemed he struggled to follow her reasoning.

'You have given an excellent reconstruction,' he said slowly. 'But it is only a hypothesis. It remains only a hypothesis unless you name the assassin and his motive.'

Sister Fidelma smiled softly.

'Very well. I was, of course, coming to that.'

She turned and let her gaze pass over their upraised faces as they watched her. Then she let her gaze rest on the haughty features of the thane of Andredswald.

Eadred interpreted her gaze as accusation and was on his feet before she had said a word, his face scowling in anger.

Ultan, the steward, moved swiftly across the room to stand before Sister Fidelma in anticipation lest Eadred let his emotions, which were clearly visible on his angry features, overcome him.

'You haven't told us the motive,' Dagobert the Frank said softly. 'Why would the thane of Andredswald murder his own cousin and prince?'

Sister Fidelma continued to stare at the arrogant Saxon.

'I have not yet said that the thane of Andredswald is the assassin,' she said softly. 'But as for motive, the motive is the very laws of the Saxon society, which, thanks be to God, are not our laws.'

Abbot Laisran was frowning.

'Explain, Fidelma. I do not understand.'

'A Saxon prince succeeds to the kingship by primogeniture. The eldest son inherits.'

Dagobert nodded impatiently.

'That is also so with our Frankish succession. But how does this provide the motive for Wulfstan's murder?'

'Two days ago a messenger from the kingdom of the South Saxons arrived here. His message was for Wulfstan. I discovered what his message was.'

'How?' demanded Raedwald. 'Royal messengers have their tongues cut out to prevent them revealing such secrets.'

Fidelma grinned.

'So you told me. Fortunately this poor man was taught to write by Diciul, the missionary of Éireann who brought Christianity and learning to your country of the South Saxons.'

'What was the message?' asked Laisran.

'Wulfstan's father had died, another victim of the Yellow Plague. Wulfstan was now king of the South Saxons and urged to return home at once.'

She glanced at Raedwald.

The big Saxon nodded silently in agreement.

'You admitted that much to me when I questioned you, Raedwald,' went on Fidelma. 'When I asked you if you liked Wulfstan you answered that it was not up to you to like or dislike your appointed king. A slip of the tongue but it alerted me to the possible motive.'

Raedwald said nothing.

'In such a barbaric system of succession, where the order of birth is the only criterion for claiming an inheritance or kingdom, there are no safeguards. In Éireann, as among our cousins in Britain, a chieftain or king not only has to be of a bloodline but has to be elected by the *derbhfine* of his family. Without such a safeguard it becomes obvious to me that only the death of a predecessor removes the obstacle of the aspirant to the throne.'

Raedwald pursed his lips and said softly: 'This is so.'

'And, with Wulfstan's death, Eadred will now succeed to the kingship?'

'Yes.'

Eadred's face was livid with anger.

'I did not kill Wulfstan!'

Sister Fidelma turned and stared deeply into his eyes.

'I believe you, for Raedwald is the assassin,' she said calmly.

Finan made a grab at Raedwald as the muscular Saxon thane sought desperately to escape from the room. Dagobert leapt forward together with Ultan, the steward, to help restrain the struggling man. When the thane of Staeningum had been overpowered, Sister Fidelma turned to the others.

'I said that the assassin had a devious mind. Yet in the attempt to lay false trails, Raedwald over-excelled himself and brought suspicion down on him. In trying to implicate Talorgen, Raedwald made a mistake and caused confusion by thinking the kerchief to be Talorgen's. It bore Dagobert's motto in Latin. Raedwald has no Latin and so did not spot his mistake. This also ruled out Eadred from suspicion as Eadred knew enough Latin to the degree that he could recognise Dagobert's motto.'

She settled her gaze on Eadred.

'If you had also been slain, then Raedwald was next in line to the kingship, was he not?'

Eadred made an affirmative gesture.

'But . . .'

'Raedwald was going to implicate you as the assassin and then show how you tried to put the blame on Talorgen. He would either have had you tried for murder under our law or, if all else failed, I doubt whether you would have returned safely to the land of the South Saxons. Perhaps you might have fallen overboard on the sea voyage. Whichever way, both Wulfstan and you would have been removed from the succession, leaving it clear for Raedwald to claim the throne.'

Eadred shook his head wonderingly. His voice was tinged with reluctant admiration.

'Never would I have suspected that a woman possessed such a meticulous mind to unravel the deviousness of this treachery in the way that you have done. I shall look upon your office with a new perspective.'

Eadred turned abruptly to the Abbot Laisran.

'I and my men will depart now, for we must return to my country. With your permission, Abbot, I shall take Raedwald with me as my prisoner. He will stand trial according to our laws and his punishment will be prescribed by them.'

Abbot Laisran inclined his head in agreement.

Eadred moved to the door, and as he did so, his eyes caught sight of Talorgen of Rheged.

'Well, *welisc*. It seems I owe you an apology for wrongly accusing you of the murder of Wulfstan. I so apologise.'

Talorgen slowly stood up, his face trying to control his surprise.

'Your apology is accepted, Saxon.'

Eadred paused and then he frowned.

'The apology notwithstanding, there can never be peace between us, *welisc*!'

Talorgen sniffed.

'The day such a peace will come is when you and your Saxon hordes will depart from the shores of Britain and return back to the land whence you came.'

Eadred stiffened, his hand going to his waist, then he paused and relaxed and almost smiled.

'Well said, *welisc*. It will never be peace!'

He strode from the room with Ultan and Dagobert leading Raedwald after him.

Talorgen turned and smiled briefly towards Sister Fidelma.

'Truly, there are wise judges among the Brehons of Ireland.'

Then he, too, was gone. Finan, the professor of law, hesitated a moment.

'Truly, now I know why your reputation is great, Fidelma of Kildare.'

Sister Fidelma gave a small sigh as he left.

'Well, Fidelma,' Abbot Laisran smiled in satisfaction,

reaching for a jug of wine, 'it seems that I have provided you with some diversion on your pilgrimage to the shrine of the Blessed Patrick at Ard Macha.'

Sister Fidelma responded to the rotund abbot's wry expression.

'A diversion, yes. Though I would have preferred something of a more pleasant nature to have occupied my time.'

The Melchester Murders

Christopher West

The Melchester Murders

It's time, now. I shall gather a few belongings together, walk slowly into town – very slowly, so I can enjoy all those things I shall never enjoy again – then commit the final act. God knows what their reaction will be when I do, but that is not in my hands. I have fulfilled my destiny; the rest is up to fate.

How did this come to be? I call it my 'vision', though I didn't actually see anything: I was sitting on a wall in the cathedral close eating my lunch, when I suddenly understood who I was and why I was here. Evil. I'd been born evil, and would die evil. I should live my life evil, too.

In that second, everything made sense – the magnificence of the architecture behind me; the goodness of Melchester's citizens going about their legitimate business; my boundless fury at these things. I had tried to live by their standards, but I was not of them or they of me. My life had seemed so passive and wasted, a blind, groping stumble down an ever-steepening slope of disasters and farewells. But all the time, it had really been an ascent. To this. I let out a great, madman's laugh; I grinned at the people who turned and stared. I would have revenge, after all!

I walked home the long way, through those new estates that had once filled me with such envy – the company cars, the flower gardens, the happily abandoned kiddies' toys. How should I put my new-found faith into practice? Crime. Some massive theft, like the crown jewels or robbing the Bank of England. What a vulgar notion! My crime would have to be something pointless, magnificently pointless, an action complete in itself with no benefit accruing to the doer. Then, and only then, it would be a true, absolute statement of faith.

I had a long debate with myself whether I could get pleasure from this act. No, I told myself, that would detract from its purity. But on the other hand, to enjoy the act would be even more evil than just to do it. I pondered this for days, then suddenly knew. Of course I could enjoy it; I should enjoy it; I would enjoy it.

And I knew at once what the act should be. I guess I'd known all along, but something inside had hidden it from me. There was no other candidate.

It was in all the papers, local and national too. And even on the TV news: his wife was there, sobbing and telling the world that Eddie had never harmed anybody, that he was the kindest man she had ever known and that she did not know how anybody could have done this. I sat watching, higher than any drugs or booze had ever taken me, on the proof of my own genius. At last! Unfortunately, the TV didn't go into the details – but the tabloid press did that next day. I've still got all the cuttings, of course: they'll find them after the arrest, when the old place is surrounded by wailing cop-cars.

'As yet, there are no clues,' the TV reporter had concluded. I remember thinking how odd that was, then realising that it must have been deliberate. The game had begun already.

In truth, the business of a 'calling card' had given me a lot of trouble. My first thought was – seriously – to have some printed with 'Son of Lucifer' on. But I soon got that out of my system. I thought of leaving a black ribbon by each victim. Subtler – but the police could go round all the shops, checking. I didn't want to make it easy for them. This was my performance; it would be on my terms from beginning to end. Then I had The Idea.

Weapons, you see, had been a problem. I'd never really been the violent kind – on the outside at least. I got bullied at school and conned at work, but I never got back at these people. This was partly out of fear, partly because the Bible says 'turn the other cheek' – dear mother, she was so religious. So I'd never actually hit anyone, let alone killed them. So I thought – firing a gun from a distance wouldn't involve any contact at all. But the police know all about guns. They can match an individual bullet to an individual weapon. And anyway, there had to be more evil ways of killing people. A knife? I really do have an aversion to them. I had to wait for The Idea, but it was worth it.

I'd already selected a victim. Edward was a commuter. I chose him from the crowd streaming out of the station in the evening – he had a particularly happy expression. I did some research, finding out about his hobbies and his favourite haunts. In the summer, he played cricket – a sport I particularly detest – and in the winter he would go jogging. Ha, ha! If Edward hadn't wanted to be so fit and healthy, he would probably still be alive now. But he chose to run along the old Roman road out of the town, up past the thicket where it was so easy to wait.

The bow and arrow had been my father's. That was its virtue: it had been sitting in an attic for twenty years. I'd never used it – hating on principle anything the old tyrant liked – but soon found it easy to operate. And shooting from the range I chose, I couldn't miss. Its only disadvantage was its size: I could be seen with it. So I always had to go to and from my place of execution under cover of darkness. It's one of the benefits of being, well, an individual, that no one misses you if you're not around. And the wait just increases the thrill of the chase.

Victim number two was female. There was nothing sexual about this: I just wanted to be fair. Donna looked so happy walking her dogs on Melchester Plain . . . Strangely, it turned out that she and Edward had known each other – always a possibility in a country town – and the cops spent quite a while working on the theory that there was some rational link between the two crimes. An unexpected bonus, looking back: all that police time wasted. But at last this line of investigation was exhausted: one day, the local paper showed the Chief Constable announcing that a madman was at loose in the town.

Sitting in my usual lunch-spot the next day was another moment of pure, transcendent triumph. Look at all those people, once so smug, now as insecure and terrified as I had once been! The bishop even preached a sermon about me inside those beautiful walls. God would have been listening; maybe he'll think again before putting people in hell here on earth.

Murder number three was a masterstroke. Numbers one and two had been in outlying places; with number three, I brought my terror right into the heart of the community. I shan't tell you how, but a teenage boy coming back from an evening at the cinema encountered some real-life action in an alley off Market Street. Unlike the other victims, he was shot from the front. The look of fear in his eyes, just for a moment! Such a promising young fellow, everyone said. What about MY promise?

The murders were now national news. A national obsession, in fact. You don't believe me? You look through my cuttings. The press are so manipulative and so sentimental – they even had a picture of Donna's dog, pining for its mistress. But in fact I was controlling them. 'Melchester is a city that lives in terror.' Dammit, I put this bloody town on the map! The police, I read one day, had called in a 'profiler' all the way from America. And – more scary – a medium from India. I needn't have worried: the medium was soon taken ill. 'Too much evil,' she said.

One day, they came. Two coppers, a constable and a sergeant. They were interviewing everyone, so it didn't mean anything. I showed them in; they sat down, their noses puckering slightly with disdain at the smell. Cleanliness is next to godliness, remember. They asked me a whole lot of questions about where I'd been and when – as if I hadn't worked all these things out ages ago! All my life I'd been terrified of policemen. Big, narrow-minded, authoritarian. Now I had them dancing to my tune. Dance, little piggies, dance! They sat there with serious looks on their faces, taking down notes, glancing around, disapproving, getting nowhere. Dance! When they left, I was so dizzy with pride that I went straight upstairs to plan number four.

I sat down and thought of suitable locations. I'd several victims in mind – time to go through the usual selection process. But I found my thoughts moving on to how I should end it all. My apotheosis; it should build and build, like a piece of beautiful music. To a climax. Where? In the cathedral, of course. I would take the bishop hostage, and hold a blunt rusty knife to his throat. I would negotiate his release, in return for – what? Yes, of course – an exclusive newspaper interview. A full-page declaration of my beliefs. And a picture of me, sweeping the cross and candles off the altar. I set to work at once.

Anne Cranfield was chosen for her voluntary work with old people, Geordie MacBride because I heard two people in a pub saying what a decent fellow he was. Not many like him around nowadays, they said. There was soon one less. That made five killings. Enough to send the town completely crazy. (It hurts, doesn't it? It's not romantic, or daring, just painful.) The police were reinforced and reinforced again: I had two more visits, during one of which they found the loose floorboard and took it up. I stood and watched, muttering about how they had to do their duty and if they caught the bastard it would be all worth it. Two days before, I'd moved the gear to a hole in the garden. But something about their attitude told me I was on their list. I shouldn't dally.

'Progress is being made.' That's what the paper said

one morning. And that evening, the Chief Constable – he'd aged about a decade since the first killing – appeared on TV saying that a 'vital' clue had been found. 'We expect to make an arrest soon,' he added. I opened the curtains a crack and stared out into the street. No one there. So were they bluffing?

I only abandoned the plan to storm the cathedral because the city was so full of coppers that I'd never get there undetected. On the morning show next day there was more chat about an impending arrest. Roadblocks had been set up around the city. I walked out to Old Hill to check, and it was true. Only one thing for it . . .

So now here we are. I'm just walking towards Castle Street – five minutes to go! I look round at the town. How much I wanted you to bring me happiness. How bitterly you let me down. But now you shall deliver your promise after all. All these people around me – the streets look fuller than they've been for ages – will all be witnesses to my last act of self-creation.

Surrender.

I turn into Castle Street. There is the blue lamp of the police station, surrounded by crowds. I'll walk up those steps, cool as ice—

'They've got him!'

A spotty-faced young man in a tie is shaking me by the hand and grinning like an ape.

'Got who?' I ask.

'The Bowman!'

'Hang him!' someone else muttered.

I quicken my pace. Everyone else is running, too. I can hear a siren: at the far end of the road, a column of cars pulls up. From one of them, two coppers get out, then a stooped figure with a sheet over his head. People shout and scream and jeer; flashbulbs pop; the figure is hustled up the steps. My steps! The Chief Constable appears and gives a short statement. A cheer goes up.

I begin to barge into the crowd, but it's too thick. 'They're MY killings, MY victims!' I tell them.

But nobody is listening.

A Little Dose of Friendship

Margaret Yorke

A Little Dose of Friendship

Mrs Wilberforce sat knitting by a window. Outside, the Atlantic Ocean spread before her, dark and mysterious, huge rollers billowing but with scarcely a whitecap to be seen. The ship rode with the sea's movement like a hobby-horse at a fair. Mrs Wilberforce had sailed, by way of Bermuda, to the United States of America and the Canadian eastern seaboard, and now the vessel in which she was a passenger was heading home.

She cruised annually, often, as this year, for a full month. In the past, she had flown to far-off areas and traversed distant seas. Expense was not a problem. At ports, she took sightseeing tours, clambering into coaches to be driven round strange cities, staring out at skyscrapers and scenic wonders, a goldfish in a bowl, seeing but not experiencing the local life. Sometimes the motion of the coach sent her to sleep, though she slept well on board, lulled like a baby in its cradle by the movements of the great white ship which carried her.

On this cruise, she shared a table in the restaurant with two couples travelling together, and Amelia. There was usually an Amelia of one kind or another on her voyages – another solitary soul. Cruises attracted solitary ladies, even solitary gentlemen, but Mrs Wilberforce sought no partner for her remaining years. What she looked for was only a little dose of friendship.

'I'm all alone,' she had told the pretty woman in the bright blue slacks and spotless white sweat-shirt who had paused beside her in the Fiesta Lounge, out of whose large windows she enjoyed looking at the ocean. She had spoken brightly, accepting her situation in the world. The pretty woman – Isobel – had asked her if she had been ashore, had described the energetic walk she and her husband had taken round the city of Quebec in brilliant, chilly autumn sunshine. She'd spoken of Montcalm and Wolfe, of artists' studios and cobbled streets, alighting like a butterfly beside Dorothy Wilberforce to point out locations on a map.

Mrs Wilberforce had dropped her statement into their talk, irrelevantly.

'You mean cruising alone?' Isobel, fortunately partnered, knew that many of the passengers were not accompanied.

'Yes – that, of course, but in every way,' said Mrs Wilberforce in a cheerful tone, picking up a stitch she had dropped, through inattention while window-gazing, in the square she was knitting to form part of a blanket for the needy. Who would sew together all those different squares, Isobel, no knitter, wondered;

the crafts organiser, whose job seemed to be a sort of occupational therapy for the passengers? 'I'm a widow,' Dorothy was adding.

'No children?' asked Isobel, wishing now that she had not stopped to chat.

'No. I had a sister, but she died last year,' said Dorothy. 'She had no children either.'

'Oh dear. I'm sorry,' said Isobel. She stood up, irresolute, not wanting to offend but not ready to listen to the story of the older woman's lonely life. 'That's sad,' she said, comforted in the knowledge that she had two sons and a daughter and the probability ahead of her, when the time was right, of grandchildren.

'It doesn't matter,' said Dorothy. 'I'm used to it.'

Why had she said that, she wondered, as Isobel, declaring she must write some postcards, moved away. This pleasant woman would not talk to her again. Meanwhile, however, Mrs Wilberforce's new and faithful friend Amelia would be there at lunch, her thin pointed nose alert as if to sniff the details of Dorothy's quiet morning, spent on board. This afternoon they were setting out together on a trip to view the autumn leaves: 'Fall Foliage', as the tour was attractively described. The itinerary was not demanding and included tea at a mountain vantage point.

Amelia, a keen walker and a lot younger than Dorothy Wilberforce, had been ashore that morning but Dorothy had not felt up to walking round the ramparts of the city, even though there was a funicular to take one to the top. Amelia would describe it all and would have bought some postcards. She'd be writing to her nephew, as she did from every port. He lived in Purley and Amelia often stayed with him and his wife Theresa, who was expecting a baby. Dorothy had liked hearing about the hardworking young couple devoted to their aunt, and she'd helped Amelia choose a soft cuddly bear for the baby.

When Amelia returned to the ship, her nose was pink from the cold outside, her eyes bright. For a disloyal instant, Dorothy was reminded of a ferret, nostrils quivering, scenting prey, then banished the reflection. Amelia was a plain woman who had missed the joys of marriage – something Dorothy had enjoyed for twenty years – and the grief of loss. Dorothy's husband had been well insured; she was, if not rich, very comfortably off, living in a large bungalow near Bournemouth. They had retired there, and two years later Jack had died, dropping dead one day while planting a new rose bush, a weeping standard, Alberic Barbier, which now thrived. Dorothy had scattered Jack's ashes round it, forking them in a little, not wanting the fragments to disperse. She had loved Jack gently and sincerely, and he'd loved her too. There had been that brief escapade with his secretary when he was in his forties; she'd watched and waited, aware of danger, doing nothing to precipitate a crisis, and gradually things had settled down. Maura had left, he'd told her, the information imparted in a throwaway manner one Friday evening just before friends invited to dinner had arrived.

'Oh,' Dorothy had answered calmly. 'That's sudden.'

'Yes,' he'd agreed, drawing the cork from a bottle of burgundy which he then set to breathe on the sideboard. 'Some family trouble. Her sister's ill.'

Dorothy had never known that Maura had a sister. She hoped the trouble was not of a more personal nature, but there were some things it was better not to know.

'I see,' she said. 'You'll miss her.'

'I'm promoting Hazel,' he had replied. Hazel worked in the typing pool. She was a plump, jolly girl in her first job; she'd lasted four years with Jack before marrying and having several babies, and she had been followed by Karen, a divorced mother of two teenagers who had remained with Jack until he retired.

Dorothy wrenched her thoughts back from the past, wherein they often strayed, and directed them to the fall foliage as she accompanied Amelia to the ship's restaurant for lunch. She consumed soup, sole, and apple crumble, then set off for the coach.

Their tour was pleasant, though Dorothy, after her good meal, dozed off once or twice and missed some of the fine vistas of golden leaves interspersed with bright splashes of scarlet from the maples. They stopped in a small village and entered a little church, whitewashed within and spare.

'How modern,' said Amelia.

'Not at all,' said Dorothy. 'It's three hundred years old.' Her response sounded tart to her own ears and she softened it by adding, 'Though I suppose that is modern, by our standards, when our churches are so much older.'

'That's what I meant,' said Amelia, apparently unruffled.

That night she went to the cabaret while Dorothy took herself off to the concert given by the professional pianist who was one of the entertainers. He played various Chopin pieces and then requests suggested by the audience. During his performance the ship began to roll and that night the seas grew rough.

Dorothy did not mind the gale, but she found

walking round the passages a problem as the vessel lurched and rocked. Her own cabin was amidships, so her discomfort was minimised by being at the centre of the axis but she knew that Amelia's, on a lower deck, was in the bow, and feared that she would suffer. Each day, Dorothy went up on deck to get some air but she did not walk about. Amelia had disappeared, absent from meals, so Dorothy telephoned her cabin to learn that she was most unwell. She did not wish to be visited; the steward was taking care of her and she would ring the doctor if she felt no better.

When she surfaced, Amelia's nose had a pale tip and her cheeks were gaunt. Dorothy advised soup and cream crackers, suggesting food might help to settle the sufferer's stomach. The seas abated to a degree and Amelia began to eat again. She went to Bingo, while Dorothy continued knitting squares, a pink one and a yellow. The blankets would be gaudy, when they were assembled; perhaps they would cheer up the recipients, the children or the elderly, thought Dorothy. She was elderly herself, and ahead lay the long winter with the garden cold and uninviting. Mr Forster, who ran the local taxi, would take her shopping once a week – she no longer drove. He would meet her when they docked.

She went to a film about San Francisco and dozed off at a crucial moment, missing the point of the story. Then the last night came.

By now the ship was in calmer waters and land was visible, to everyone's relief. Farewells were exchanged, addresses written down. Dorothy thought it was rather like the end of term. Some of the crew, including several of the entertainers, were going home; they were excited and happy.

'Goodbye, Amelia. We'll keep in touch,' said Dorothy, who did not mean to do so. Shipboard acquaintances were better kept as such, with perhaps a Christmas card the first year and then silence.

She thought she might not cruise again. All those white heads and walking sticks depressed her, and she worried about the stewards and crew, most of them from India or other countries where poverty was endemic: what did they feel about the extravagance and waste, the endless courses on the menu, the heaped-up plates of those using the buffet on the deck? Greedy passengers ate in a day enough to keep an impoverished family for a week. But their fares paid the crew's wages.

Donating the sum she had spent on this holiday to a charity could have been a better use for the money, Dorothy reflected, closing up the holdall which contained her toilet things and nightdress. On the other hand, she had been looked after and had company, surely worthwhile ends in themselves, but what use was she to anyone?

Such thoughts were negative. She turned her mind towards home, to the prospect of Mr Forster carrying in her luggage and Linda Cherry, her cleaning lady, brewing coffee – really good, fresh coffee. She'd bought a soapstone polar bear and a bottle of duty-free scent for Linda, and whisky for Mr Forster, who liked a nip. Perhaps, next year, she'd spend a week in Cornwall, in a good hotel.

The passengers disembarked in sections, upper decks first. Dorothy looked for Mr Forster, who would have had to park his black Granada in the pound and claim her on foot before being allowed to drive in and collect her.

She could not see him. Cars and taxis were coming and

going; happy reunions were achieved; and people got into cars which had been left with a local garage who returned them to the dockside for this moment. None of those looking about for passengers was Mr Forster. Then she saw a man holding a large card bearing the name MRS DOROTHY WILBERFORCE.

She wasn't Mrs Dorothy Wilberforce. She was still Mrs Jack Wilberforce. Dorothy had been proud of that position, the status it had granted her. Before she married Jack she had been a bank clerk, and had not considered herself high in the pecking order. However, for practical purposes, these days, such niceties were of no account, and, tentatively, she approached.

The man, who was about thirty, thickset, with sandy hair clipped very short, wore a chauffeur's cap and dark jacket. He stepped forward as she approached and said, 'Mrs Wilberforce of Poplar Lodge?'

'Yes,' said Dorothy. 'Where's Mr Forster?'

'He's broken his leg,' said the man. 'I'm helping him out. Ron Baldwin's the name.'

'Oh,' said Dorothy. 'I see. Poor Mr Forster.'

'These your bags?' asked Ron, and he picked up her two cases, one of which ran on wheels. Despite the rules, his car was parked nearby.

'Yes,' said Dorothy. 'Thank you.'

Ron stowed them in the boot of the car – a grey Sierra – helping Mrs Wilberforce into the rear seat and aiding her as she secured the seat belt, then slid behind the wheel.

'How did Mr Forster break his leg?' she asked, as Ron drove swiftly out of the dock area.

'It was a road accident,' said Ron. 'He stepped in front of a car which didn't stop.'

'Oh dear! Where was this?' asked Mrs Wilberforce.

'At his garage. It was very dark – a moonless night. The car reversed away from one of the pumps instead of going forward.'

As well as running a taxi, Mr Forster did repairs and sold petrol, employing one lad to help him.

'How dreadful. Is he in hospital?'

'He is, and he'll be there a while yet, all tied up to ropes and pulleys,' Ron informed her.

'Traction. It must be bad,' said Mrs Wilberforce.

Ron did not reply, concentrating on accelerating as they passed the city limits and reached the open countryside. Sunlight slanted amongst the trees, oaks and beeches and a few surviving elms. The fall foliage here was just as lovely as the spectacle she had seen across the Atlantic, thought Mrs Wilberforce; it was simply on a smaller scale. She sat silent; already her return was not as she expected, but Linda Cherry would be waiting for her when she reached home. She clung to that thought until Ron spoke again.

'Mrs Cherry has had to leave you,' he said. 'She's ever so sorry, but there it is. She's been offered a full-time job elsewhere and she couldn't afford to turn it down, but she's made arrangements for you. My auntie will be helping out. I'll be bringing her to see you this afternoon.'

Helping out, he'd said, just as he was helping out Mr Forster.

'I see,' said Mrs Wilberforce, who didn't see at all. Linda Cherry had been with her for years, coming twice a week to clean the house and polish the silver. She went also to another house near by, and professed herself content with these two jobs. She simply liked to earn enough to feel independent and provide a treat or two for herself and Fred, who was a bus driver. They had one daughter, still at school, the apple of their eye.

As if to match Mrs Wilberforce's change of mood, the sky grew dark and it began to rain. To and fro went the Sierra's wipers as her spirits sank. No Mr Forster, and now no Linda, but instead of them, Ron and his unknown auntie. She sat quietly, trying to adjust as they drove along. After a while, Ron removed his chauffeur's cap and laid it beside him on the passenger's seat. Then he turned on the radio, and pop music was relayed to Mrs Wilberforce's unwilling ears, but she did not like to protest. Anyway, the noise prevented conversation; she did not want to hear news of other changes.

After past cruises, she had regaled Mr Forster with tales of her travels, descriptions of ports visited and the people she had met. Now there was nothing to say. She stared at the back of Ron's head, where the fair hair sprang strongly from his thick red neck. His ears were large, with big pendant lobes. She had never liked large ears. Looking away from this alien sight, she caught his eye in the driving mirror and glanced quickly away; his expression was almost sly, she thought, annoyed that he had noticed her interest.

After today, they need not meet again. Mr Forster would recover. There was the weekly shopping, though: would Ron expect to take her? She need not employ him; there were several taxi firms in the area. But would Mr Forster lose income if she hired someone else? And there was the aunt. Well, she need not decide about either of them now. She closed her eyes and briefly dozed, waking when Ron braked suddenly as he cut in past a cruising Rover Montego on the dual carriageway. After that she sat tensely, aware that he was not as careful a driver as Mr Forster.

At Poplar Lodge, he waited while she found her key and unlocked the front door, then took her bags in, just as Mr Forster always did. She wrote him a cheque, and he asked her to make it out to him, which seemed reasonable as he had done the journey in what was, presumably, his own car. It was only after he left, and Dorothy was starting to unpack, that she realised he had taken her luggage to her bedroom without being told which door to open. How had he known where to go?

Tired and depressed, she dismissed the question as foolish and went into the kitchen to make coffee. This was the moment when Linda Cherry should have been there, hiding her expectancy, waiting for the present her employer would certainly have bought for her. Mrs Wilberforce settled for instant coffee and, because breakfast on the ship had been early, nibbled a digestive biscuit which she did not finish. Somehow, it had no flavour. She returned to finish her unpacking, a task Linda had always helped her with before, folding tissue paper and hanging up the black evening skirt and array of blouses which were the answers to problems of attire for nights of varying formality.

There was mail waiting, some bills and circulars, but no personal letters; so many of Mrs Wilberforce's contemporaries had died that nowadays she received few letters that were not to do with business – her stocks and shares, her pension, her statements from the bank. She sat at her desk and wrote cheques, addressed envelopes and stamped them; she would take them to the letter box on the corner in the morning, if the postman did not call. He would always take them for her when he visited the house.

After this she felt tired and decided to lie down. She'd had no lunch, but she wanted none. She might thaw out a frozen meal this evening, and watch television; that would pass the time. In bed, under the quilt, her skirt off and her shoes placed neatly on the floor, she fell asleep, forgetting about Ron and his aunt, due that afternoon.

A sound woke her. Her legs were no longer strong and she needed spectacles, but her hearing was still acute. What she had heard was the front door opening. Who could it be? Only Linda Cherry had a key. Perhaps she had come to explain her abrupt departure. Mrs Wilberforce sat up, clutching the quilt to her thin chest, and she heard the sound of voices from the hall, first a man's and then a woman's.

With a pang of dismay, she remembered Ron's promise to bring round his aunt, but they would ring the bell. These were burglars, imagining that she was still away. She was stretching out her hand to lift the telephone when the bedroom door was opened.

'Well, dear, isn't this nice?' said Amelia from the ship, her thin nose pinker than ever as she entered the room, smiling what Dorothy Wilberforce now saw was a Judas smile. 'Ron said you'd be needing some help, and here I am. I'm sure you'd appreciate a nice cup of tea. Ron's just putting the kettle on.' She advanced and stood looking down at Dorothy. 'Just rest, my dear,' she instructed. 'Your worries are all over. We'll take care of everything. Ron's my nephew,' she added, superfluously.

*

When Linda Cherry received a letter from Mrs Wilberforce, written from the ship, saying that her services would no longer be required, she was most upset. The letter stated that on the cruise Mrs Wilberforce had met a very pleasant lady who, when they returned, would be moving into Poplar Lodge as a companion-help. There was not even a cheque in lieu of notice, which was unlike Mrs Wilberforce, who had always been most generous. Linda was bitterly hurt. So was Mr Forster, who also received a letter. His told him not to meet her at the port as a friend would give her a lift home. He and Linda Cherry did not compare notes with one another as, whilst Linda lived one mile from Poplar Lodge, Mr Forster's garage was two miles in the other direction. Eventually they met when Linda stopped to fill her car with petrol at Mr Forster's pump, and by then they had both decided that if this was the way Mrs Wilberforce wanted things, so be it. Linda found another job and Mr Forster, his legs undamaged, carried on as normal.

Mrs Wilberforce's bills were paid, her dividends were received, and a letter authorising Amelia Dixon to cash cheques on her account was accepted by the bank. Mrs Wilberforce's signature was witnessed by Ron Baldwin. A grey Sierra car went, unremarked, in and out of Poplar Lodge. It was succeeded by a blue Mercedes. The bungalow was screened from the road by banks of trees and shrubs; comings and goings were not observed by neighbours, although a blonde woman in a white Porsche was sometimes seen and occasionally there seemed to be late parties.

A letter stating that Mrs Wilberforce's account was overdrawn came from the bank, with a request that she make an appointment to see the manager. Amelia telephoned, speaking on behalf of Dorothy Wilberforce and saying that matters would be attended to as soon as she had recovered from an attack of influenza. After this, boards went up outside the house, advertising it for sale.

Isobel saw them when, a year after meeting Mrs Wilberforce on the cruise, she drove that way after a visit to friends in the neighbourhood. She had suddenly remembered the pleasant, lonely old woman she had seen standing on a verandah, a little forlorn, staring at the autumn leaves from the viewpoint at the foot of the Laurentian mountains. Isobel had felt guilty at abandoning the woman earlier that day in the ship's lounge and had sought to make amends. They had had tea together in the timbered clubhouse at the golf course which was the spot from which they gazed upon the foliage. Golf carts bearing happy players trundled past the window as they drank tea and ate shortcake. Isobel's husband was not there; he had met a business friend in Quebec, leaving her to take the excursion without him. Later, before the ship docked, she had obtained Mrs Wilberforce's address and had sent her a Christmas card, though she had not received one in return, but you shouldn't expect too much from the old. She remembered that Dorothy had said she was alone in the world, without even, it seemed, a cousin.

She decided to pay her a call. It wouldn't take up much time.

The bungalow could not be seen from the road. Isobel recalled Mrs Wilberforce mentioning the garden; she had been fond of it, and her roses. Hadn't she mentioned a weeping Alberic Barbier? Isobel, a woman who kept her word, had not ignored Mrs Wilberforce during the remainder of the cruise; they had had brief chats in the Fiesta Lounge, and on deck, braving the Atlantic gale. Now, Isobel saw the For Sale boards by the gates, then the neglected state of the place, the long grass on either side of the drive, the overgrown rose bushes. There was a straggling Iceberg, loaded with withered blooms. From the car, she could not see the Alberic Barbier. Wasn't it yellow? It might have ceased blooming now; most of the roses were over.

Had Mrs Wilberforce died? Was that why the house was for sale? It was possible: she must have been about eighty.

Filled with foreboding, Isobel parked the car and got out. The curtains hung limply at the blank windows which were, she saw, rather dirty. On the ship, Mrs Wilberforce had always been well dressed. She was, though old, elegant, and not the type of person to tolerate an untidy garden and grubby windows.

Increasingly uneasy, Isobel rang the bell, and after some delay the door was opened by a young woman in leopard-like leggings and a gold-spangled knitted tunic. She wore high-heeled shoes, and several flashy bracelets jangled on both wrists as she took a cigarette from her mouth in order to speak.

'Yes?' she said. 'Have you come to see the house? Appointments have to be made through the agent.'

'Mrs Wilberforce is dead, then,' said Isobel flatly. 'Who are you?' She couldn't be a niece or a granddaughter; there were none.

'Who's Mrs Wilberforce?' asked the young woman.

'This is her house,' said Isobel firmly. 'Or it was a year ago.'

She knew she had come to the right place: the name, Poplar Lodge, had been visible on a board by the gate.

'Oh, you mean Ron's old gran, do you? Yes, she's dead, poor old thing,' said the woman.

But there had been no grandson Ron. What could the woman mean?

'When did she die?' asked Isobel. 'What of?'

'I don't know. You'll have to ask Ron. She left him the house and everything, but we're selling up. It's too quiet here,' said the woman.

'You're Ron's wife?' Isobel uttered the question carefully. Something was very wrong here, or else Mrs Wilberforce had been playing for sympathy, professing an isolation that did not exist.

'Not exactly,' said the woman, and laughed. 'It's only a bit of paper, isn't it? Common law, it's called. Ron's out. I'll tell him you came.' But she did not ask Isobel's name.

'It doesn't matter,' said Isobel, now anxious to get away. 'Where does Mrs Cherry live?' she asked, as she turned to go.

'Never heard of her,' said the woman.

There were such things as telephone directories. Isobel got back into her VW Golf and drove carefully down the drive to the gates. As she went, she saw the umbrella shape of the weeping rose in the unkempt grass at the side of what had once been the lawn. Five minutes after she left, Ron, in his Mercedes, returned.

Isobel traced Linda Cherry. There were several Cherrys in the directory and she tried three before finding the one who had worked for Mrs Wilberforce for so many years. Dorothy Wilberforce had mentioned her when

Isobel, waiting to disembark from the ship, had enquired if there would be someone to help her when she reached home. Thank goodness she had remembered the name; it was a pretty one; she had said so when she heard it and Dorothy had said that Linda was a pretty woman.

'Well, pleasant-looking, really,' she amended. 'I'm fond of her.'

Tracked down, Linda suggested that Isobel should come straight round to Number Six, Parson's Way, where she lived, and she gave directions. Soon, Isobel was sitting in Linda's lounge with a cup of tea and a piece of gingerbread while Linda described how upset she had been at her sudden dismissal and how, using Christmas as her excuse, she had gone to Poplar Lodge with a card and a home-baked sponge cake such as Mrs Wilberforce so enjoyed. The door had been opened by a thin-faced woman with a pointed nose, the new companion, who had said that Mrs Wilberforce was resting and could see no one that day. She had accepted the cake and the card, but there had been no acknowledgement, no note of thanks nor a telephone call. Linda had not repeated her visit.

'She had no relations,' Isobel said.

'That's right,' said Linda. 'No one at all, and her friends had died. It gets ever so lonely when you're old.'

'Yes,' agreed Isobel, and shivered suddenly. 'But that woman who answered the door said that Mrs Wilberforce was her partner's grandmother. She's dead,' she added. 'Dorothy Wilberforce, I mean. She left everything to Ron, this woman said, and they're selling up because it's so quiet.'

'But that's not right,' said Linda. 'We'd have known if she'd died, surely? Or Mr Forster would. He often helps out the undertaker.'

'Who's Mr Forster?'

'The taxi. He drove her such a lot, but he was told not to meet her off the boat,' Linda said. 'A friend was giving her a lift, she said, in a note.'

But Isobel remembered mention of a taxi.

'What friend?' she wanted to know, and Linda could not tell her.

Isobel had to return home that night, but she came back two days later and visited Mr Forster. She called, also, at the office of the estate agent who was handling the sale of Poplar Lodge. Linda Cherry knew which doctor looked after Mrs Wilberforce, and Isobel went to the surgery, but she received a dusty answer there because patients' affairs were sacrosanct. A nurse, however, admitted that Mrs Wilberforce had not been seen for more than a year, which was surprising, as she often got bad colds in the winter and usually needed a little attention.

'I'm going to the police,' said Isobel. 'If there's nothing wrong, they'll tell us, and if there is, the sooner it's discovered the better.'

Since Isobel was not a relative, the police took some convincing that there was cause for concern, but Linda knew where Mrs Wilberforce kept her bank account, and a detective was able to discover that cheques had been cashed for more than a year by an authorised person, Amelia Dixon, and later by a Ronald Baldwin. Signatures had seemed to be authentic; such arrangements were quite customary for the elderly and there had been no occasion to question the practice. However, Mrs Wilberforce had been spending more freely than in years past, the bank finally conceded, not revealing that she was in debt.

An inspector and a woman officer went round to Poplar Lodge where a man opened the door to them and told them that Mrs Wilberforce was away on her annual cruise. Meanwhile, he was looking after the place, which was up for sale. She was moving into sheltered accommodation, he declared. The inspector asked for the name of the ship, and when told, made contact with the cruise line, to learn that no passenger of that name was registered at present. The vessel was now in the South Pacific.

By the time the inspector and his colleague, with two uniformed officers, returned to Poplar Lodge, Ron had gone; so had the woman whom Isobel had met, and they had stripped the place of every bit of furniture. It was quite empty; curtains and carpets had been removed: everything that had marked a life had vanished.

The bodies were found in the garden. Mrs Wilberforce's was close to the rose tree that had thrived on her husband's ashes; it was naked, and ringless, in an advanced state of decomposition and identified by her dentist. Amelia's was near the lily pond and it had been disposed of more recently. A large quantity of barbiturate was found in the remains, and there were signs of suffocation, possibly by means of a plastic bag. The cause of Mrs Wilberforce's death was more difficult to establish, but because of the method of disposal, foul play was a near certainty. Traces of barbiturate were later found, and fragments of wool, proved to come from a sweater which was on the corpse of Amelia, were found around the hands, as if Mrs Wilberforce had dragged at the wearer's garment as she lost consciousness, perhaps was held down by Amelia.

It took patience and many interviews to piece the story together. Amelia – whom Isobel identified from a photograph taken aboard the ship – had befriended Dorothy Wilberforce and learned of her solitary state. She had taken Dorothy's doorkey at some point – perhaps offering to mind her handbag while Dorothy visited the library – and had had another cut in Quebec, then sent this back to Ron Baldwin who was genuinely her nephew, in a letter innocently carried by a dancer from the ship's entertainment troupe who flew back to England from Montreal. Amelia had also written to Linda Cherry and to Mr Forster, and enclosed the letters with the key so that Ron posted them all in England. She had had ample opportunity to practise Dorothy Wilberforce's signature, which she had copied from the charge card carried on board. This had been enough, too, to secure the arrangements at the bank and to effect other business deals, for Ron had been able to witness his aunt's forgeries. Amelia saw no reason why they should not live out the rest of their lives at Poplar Lodge, but Ron had broken up with his never-pregnant wife, the blonde with the Porsche, seen occasionally at first. There had been payments to her to keep her quiet; then his new girl-friend had been extravagant and greedy. She had known nothing about Amelia.

If he'd managed to sell the house before Isobel's visit, he might have got away with it.

'Or if you'd never called,' said Linda Cherry, who

was wishing she had been more persistent, though it was clear that Mrs Wilberforce had been murdered almost at once after her return from the fatal cruise.

'Or if you'd done nothing about it,' said Mr Forster. This was after Dorothy's belated funeral at the local church.

'They'd have been found out in the end,' said Isobel. 'The bank would have got suspicious eventually, or some business transaction would have needed investigating.'

But they didn't catch Ron until his estranged wife realised, from the newspaper reports about the bodies in the garden, that he had killed his own aunt, and she shopped him.

Biographical Notes on the Contributors

Robert Barnard has spent most of his adulthood behind a desk, either marking student essays or writing detective novels, but since he has mostly done this abroad (first in Australia, then in Norway) people often comment on his adventurous life. He has now moved back to the United Kingdom, lives in Leeds, and still spends much of his life behind a desk. He also spends part of his life as Barnard Bastable.

Brian Battison was born in Northampton. Before becoming a writer, he was an actor, winning gold medals at the London Academy of Music and Dramatic Art and appearing on stage with the Birmingham Repertory Theatre and on television. His first novel, *The Christmas Bow Murder*, was published in January 1994, and his second, *Fool's Ransom*, in September 1994.

James Hamilton-Paterson, past winner of the Newdigate Prize for Poetry at Oxford, more recently won the Whitbread First Novel Award with *Gerontius*. He has achieved considerable critical acclaim since with *Seven-Tenths* and *Grief Work*. He divides his time between Tuscany and the Philippines.

Bill James, is the pseudonym of James Tucker. As Bill James he writes the successful Harper and Iles police procedurals. He also writes espionage and crime as David Craig, and his novel *Whose Little Girl Are You?* was filmed by Warner Bros as *The Squeeze*. Under his own name, he has written novels and a critical study of novelist Anthony Powell. He lives near Cardiff.

Nancy Livingston has worked as an actress, a cook, a musician, an air stewardess and as a production assistant in television. She is the author of four bestselling historical romances, eight crime novels and radio plays. She has been Chairman of the Crime Writers' Association and currently lives in Suffolk with her husband.

Ian Rankin is the creator of the highly acclaimed Inspector John Rebus novels. He now lives in France, a far cry from his native Edinburgh, where he finds that distance has made the fictional exploits of Rebus even more inventive.

Julian Symons waits for the sound of the dreaded word *doyen* when introduced at dinner or at parties. Awarded the Cartier/Crime Writers' Association Diamond Dagger in 1990, he is a revered critic, biographer, poet and man of letters as well as crime novelist.

Peter Tremayne, born in Coventry in 1943, is the author of twenty-one novels and two short story collections in the fantasy genre. Many of his books have been published on both sides of the Atlantic and in translation. The *Literary Review* has said of his work: 'He has the useful ability to meld gripping situation with solidly researched background detail without disturbing the narrative flow'. He has just started to write a series of Dark Age 'whodunnit' tales featuring Sister Fidelma. Because of the authenticity of the background, it may come as no surprise that Peter Tremayne is the pseudonym of the well-known Celtic scholar and author Peter Berresford Ellis.

Christopher West was born in 1954. He did a variety of jobs from postman to stockbroker's assistant, then went to the London School of Economics as a mature student, gaining a First in Philosophy. His first book, *Journey to the Middle Kingdom*, was published in 1991; his second, *Dragon*, and his third, *The Death of a Blue Lantern*, have recently been published. He lives in north Herefordshire.

Margaret Yorke was a driver in the WRNS for the last three years of the War. She was the first woman ever to work in Christ Church Library, Oxford. Her recreations are the theatre, reading, music, gardening and travel. Her thought-provoking and highly acclaimed novels hinge on the effect extraordinary events have on ordinary people. She now lives in Buckinghamshire.